P9-CMZ-672

LITTLE
MISUNDERSTANDINGS
OF NO IMPORTANCE

ALSO BY ANTONIO TABUCCHI

LETTER FROM CASABLANCA
(Translated by Janice M. Thresher)

LITTLE MISUNDERSTANDINGS OF NO IMPORTANCE

STORIES BY ANTONIO TABUCCHI

TRANSLATED BY
FRANCES FRENAYE

A NEW DIRECTIONS BOOK

© Giangiacomo Feltrinelli Editore Milano, 1985
Translation copyright © 1987 by Frances Frenaye

All rights reserved. Except for brief passages quoted in a newspaper, magazine, radio, or television review, no part of this book may be reproduced
in any form or by any means, electronic or mechanical, including photo-
copying and recording, or by any information storage and retrieval system
without permission in writing from the Publisher.

Published by arrangement with Giangiacomo Feltrinelli Editore, Milan
Manufactured in the United States of America
This translation of *Piccoli equivoci senza importanza* first published
clothbound by New Directions in 1987
The lines from *Antigone* on page 4 are translated from the Greek by F. S.
Storr.
The translations from Baudelaire's *Paris Spleen* in "Any Where Out of
the World" are by Louise Varèse.

Library of Congress Cataloging-in-Publication Data

Tabucchi, Antonio, 1943–
    Little misunderstandings of no importance.
    Translation of: Piccoli equivoci senza importanza.
    I. Title.
PQ4880.A24P5313   1987   853'.914   87-1578

ISBN 0-8112-1029-4

New Directions Books are published for James Laughlin
by New Directions Publishing Corporation
80 Eighth Avenue, New York 10011

CONTENTS

NOTE

Baroque writers loved ambiguity. Calderón, and others with him, made ambiguity into a metaphor for the world. I suppose that they were moved by faith that, on the day when we awaken from the dream of living, our earthly ambiguity will finally be explained.

I, too, speak of ambiguities, but it's not so much that I like them; I am driven, rather, to seek them out. Misunderstandings, uncertainties, belated understandings, useless remorse, treacherous memories, stupid and irredeemable mistakes, all these irresistibly fascinate me, as if they constituted a vocation, a sort of lowly stigmata. The fact that the attraction is mutual is not exactly a consolation. I might be consoled by the conviction that life is by nature ambiguous and distributes ambiguities among all of us. But this would be, perhaps, a presumptuous axiom, not unlike the baroque metaphor.

Concerning the stories collected here, I should like to supply only a few notes on their beginnings. I stole *A Riddle* in Paris one evening in 1975, and it stayed within me long enough to come out in a version that unfortunately betrays the original. I shouldn't mind if *Spells* and *Any Where in the World* were considered, in the broadest sense of the term, ghost stories, which doesn't mean that they can't have another interpretation. The first owes something to a theory of the French child psychologist Dr. Françoise Dolto, while, in the case of the second, it may be superfluous to specify that it was inspired by Baudelaire's *Le spleen de Paris*, particularly the prose poem from which I took the title. *Bitterness and Clouds* is a realistic story. *Cinema* owes much to a rainy evening, a small railway station on the Riviera, and to the face of an actress now dead.

About the rest of the stories I have little to add. I can only say that I wish *Waiting for Winter* had been written by Henry James and *The Trains that Go to Madras* by Rudyard Kipling. They would doubtless have come off better that way. Rather than regret for what I have written, I feel regret for what I shall never be able to read.

—*Antonio Tabucchi*

LITTLE MISUNDERSTANDINGS
OF NO IMPORTANCE

The clerk called the court to order and there was a brief silence as the nearly white-haired Federico, in his judge's robe, led the little procession through the side door into the courtroom. At that very moment the tune of *Dusty Road* surged up in my mind. I watched them take their seats as if I were witnessing a ritual, remote and incomprehensible, but projected into the future. The image of those solemn men, sitting on a bench with a crucifix hanging over it, faded into the image of a past which, like an old film, was my present. Almost mechanically my hand scribbled *Dusty Road*, while my thoughts travelled backwards. Leo, confined like a dangerous animal in the prisoner's cage, lost his sickly, unhappy look. I saw him leaning on his grandmother's Empire-style console with that old bored and knowing expression which made for his very special charm. "Tonino," he was saying, "put *Dusty Road* on again, will you?" And I put the record back on. Yes, Leo deserved to dance with Maddalena, known as the Tragic Muse because as Antigone in the school play she had broken into uncontrollable sobs. This was the appropriate record, yes it was, for dancing so passionately in the drawing room of Leo's grandmother. Here were the antecedents of the trial, that evening when Leo and Fede-

1

rico had taken turns dancing with the auburn-haired Tragic
Muse, gazing into her eyes and swearing that they weren't
rivals, that they didn't give a damn for her. They were dancing
for the sake of dancing, that was all. But they were mad about
her, of course, and so was I as I changed the records, looking
as if I didn't care.

From one dance to another a year went by, a year marked by
a certain phrase, one that we ran into the ground because it
fitted any and every occasion. Missing an appointment,
spending money you didn't have in the bank, forgetting a
solemn promise, finding a highly recommended book a total
bore, all these mistakes and ambiguities were described as
"little misunderstandings of no importance". The original
example was something that happened to Federico and roused
us to memorable gales of laughter. Federico, like the rest of us,
had planned his future and signed up for Classics; he was
already a whiz at Greek and had played the part of Creon in
Antigone. We, instead, had opted for Modern Literature. "It's
closer to us," said Leo, "and you can't compare James Joyce
with those boring ancients, can you?" We were at the Caffè
Goliardico, the students' meeting place, each of us with his
registration book, looking over the schedule of courses,
stretched out on the billiard table. Memmo had joined us; he
was a fellow from Lecce with political commitments and
anxious that politics be handled "the way it should be", so we
called him "Little Pol" and the nickname stuck throughout
the year. At a certain point Federico appeared on the scene,
looking very upset and waving his registration book in the
air. He was so breathless and beside himself that he was barely
able to explain. They had signed him up, by mistake, for Law
and he simply couldn't get over it. To give him moral support
we went with him to the administrative office, where we
tangled with an amiable but indifferent old codger who had
dealt with thousands of students over the years. He looked
carefully at Federico's book and then at his worried face. "Just

a little misunderstanding that can't be corrected," he said. "No use worrying about it." Federico stared at him in dismay, his cheeks reddening. "A little misunderstanding that can't be corrected?" he stammered. The old man did not lose his composure. "Sorry," he said, "that's not what I meant. I meant a little misunderstanding of no importance. I'll get it fixed for you before Christmas. Meanwhile, if you like, you can take the Law courses. That way you won't be wasting your time." We went away choking with laughter: a little misunderstanding of no importance! And Federico's angry look made us laugh all the more.

Strange, the way things happen. One morning a few weeks later, Federico turned up at the café looking quite pleased with himself. He had just come out of a class on the philosophy of law, where he had gone merely to pass the time, and well, boys, believe it or not, he'd grasped certain problems he'd never grasped before. The Greek tragedians, by comparison, had nothing to say. He already knew the classics, anyhow, so he'd decided to stay with Law.

Federico the judge said something in a questioning tone; his voice sounded faraway and metallic as if it were coming through a telephone. Time staggered and took a vertical fall, and the face of Maddalena, ringed by tiny bubbles, floated in a puddle of years. Perhaps it's not such a good idea to go and see a girl you've been in love with on the day they're amputating her breasts. If only in self-defence. But I had no wish to defend myself; I'd long since surrendered. And so I hung about in the hall outside the operating room, where patients are made to wait for their turn. She was wheeled in, wearing on her face the innocently happy look of pre-anesthesia, which I've heard stirs up a sort of unconscious excitement. There was an element of fear, I could see, but dulled by drugs. Should I say something? What I wanted to say was: "Maddalena, I was always in love with you; I don't know why I've never managed to tell you before." But you can't say such a thing to a girl entering the operating room for an operation like that. Instead I broke out at full speed with some lines from *Antigone*, which I'd spoken in the performance years before:

> "Many wonders there be, but naught more wondrous than man,
> Over the surging sea, with a whitening south wind wan,
> Through the foam of the firth man makes his perilous way."

God knows how they came to mind so exactly, and whether she remembered them, whether she was in a condition to understand, but she squeezed my hand before they wheeled her away. I went down to the hospital coffee-shop, where the only alcohol was Ramazzotti Bitters and it took a dozen glasses to get me drunk. When I began to feel a bit queasy I went and sat on a bench in front of the hospital, telling myself that it would be quite mad to seek out the surgeon, a madness born of drink. Because I wanted to find the surgeon and ask him not to throw those breasts into the incinerator but to give them to me. I wanted to keep them, and even if they were rotten inside I didn't care; there's something rotten in all of us and I cared for those breasts—how could I put it?—they had a special meaning for me; I hoped he understood. But a flicker of reason stopped me; I managed to get a taxi and go home, where I slept through the afternoon. It was dark when the telephone woke me—I didn't notice the time. Federico was on the line saying: "Tonino, it's me. Can you hear, Tonino? It's me." "Where are you?" I asked in gummy voice. "I'm down south, in Catanzaro." "Catanzaro? What are you doing there?" "I'm trying for the post of prosecutor. I've heard that Maddalena's ill, in the hospital." "Exactly. Do you remember those breasts of hers? Well, snip, snip, they're gone." "What are you saying, Tonino. Are you drunk?" "Of course I'm drunk, drunk as a drunk, and life makes me sick, and you make me sick, too, taking an exam there in Catanzaro. Why didn't you marry her, tell me that? She was in love with you, not with Leo, and you knew it; you didn't marry her because you were afraid. And why the devil did you marry that know-it-all wife of yours, tell me that! You're a bastard, Federico!" There was a click as he hung up. I muttered a few more expletives into the telephone, then went back to bed and dreamed of a field of poppies.

And so the years continued to flutter back and forth, as they passed, while Leo and Federico continued to dance with Maddalena in the Empire-style drawing room. In the space of a second, just as in an old film, while they sat in the courtroom, the one wearing his judge's robe, the other in the prisoner's cage, the merry-go-round turned, leaves flew off the calendar and stuck to one another, and they danced with Maddalena, gazing into her eyes, while I changed the records. Up came a summer we all spent together in the mountain camp of the National Olympics Committee, the walks in the woods and the contagious passion for tennis. The only serious player was Leo, with his unbeatable backhand, his good looks, close-fitting T-shirt, glossy hair, and the towel wound casually around his neck when the game was over. In the evening we stretched out on the grass and talked of one thing and another, wondering on whose chest Maddalena would lay her head. And then a winter that took us all by surprise. First of all on account of Leo. Who could have imagined him, so well turned out and so ostentatiously futile, with an arm around the statue in the hallway leading to the university president's office, haranguing the students. He wore a very becoming olive-green parka, military style. I'd bought a blue one, which I thought went better with my eyes, but Maddalena didn't notice, or at least didn't say so. She was intent on Federico's parka, which was too big, with dangling sleeves and was bunched up round his ramrod body in a ridiculous fashion which, for some reason, was appealing to women.

Now Leo started to talk in his low-pitched, monotonous voice, as if he were telling a story, in the ironical manner that I knew so well. In the courtroom you could have heard a pin

drop; the newspaper reporters hunched over their notes as if
he were telling the Great Secret, and Federico, too, followed
him intently. Good God, I thought, why must you pretend to
follow so closely? What he's saying isn't so strange; that
winter you were in on it, too. I almost imagined Federico
standing up and saying: "Gentlemen of the jury, with your
permission, I'd like to tell this part myself, because I knew it
at first hand. The bookshop was called Nuovo Mondo; it was
on the Piazza Dante where now, if I'm not mistaken, there's a
smart shop which sells perfumes and Gucci bags. It had a
large room, with a closet, a smaller room and a toilet on the
right side. We never kept explosives in the small room, only
the strawberries Memmo brought up from Apulia after he had
been there on vacation. Every evening, in season, we got
together to eat strawberries and olives. The chief topic of
conversation was the Cuban Revolution—there was a poster
of Che Guevara over the cash register—but we talked about
revolutions of the past as well. As a matter of fact, I was the
one to talk about them. My friends had no historical or philosophical background, whereas I was studying for an exam on
political ideas (which I passed with top marks). And so I gave
them lessons—seminars, we called them—on Babeuf, Ba-
kunin, and Carlo Cattaneo. Actually revolutions didn't really
interest me. I did it because I was in love with a red-haired girl
called Maddalena. I was sure she was in love with Leo, or,
rather, I knew she was in love with me but I was afraid she was
in love with Leo. In short, it was a little misunderstanding of
no importance, a phrase popular with us at the time. And Leo
was always making fun of me; he had a gift for that. He was
witty and ironical and plied me with tricky catch questions
which conveyed the idea that I was a liberal but he was a true
radical, a revolutionary. He wasn't all that radical, really; he
put it on in order to impress Maddalena, but whether it was by
chance or from conviction, he took on a prominent role and
became the most important member of our group. Yet, for

him, too, this was a little misunderstanding which he considered of no importance. And then you know how it is: the roles that we assume become real. In life things easily get locked in, and an attitude freezes into a choice.

But Federico said none of these things. He was listening attentively to the prosecutor's questions and Leo's answers. It's not possible, I thought to myself; it's all a play. But it wasn't a play; it was real. Leo was on trial; the things he had done were real and he was admitting to them, impassively, while Federico impassively listened. He couldn't do otherwise, I realized, because that was his role in the comedy that they were playing. At this point I was moved by an impulse to rebel, to interfere, to erase the prepared script and rewrite it. What could I do? I wondered, and the only recourse, it occurred to me, was Memmo; yes, that was the only thing to do. I went out of the courtroom, showing my press card to the *carabinieri*. In the hallway, while I was dialling the number, I racked my brain for what I was going to say. They're going to sentence Leo, I'd tell him; come quickly, because you've got to do something. He's digging his own grave; it's totally absurd. Yes, he's guilty, I know, but not to that extent; he's just a cog in a machine that's crushed him. He's pretending he was at the controls, but that's just in order to live up to his reputation. He's never manipulated any machine and perhaps there's no proof of what he's saying. He's just Leo, the Leo that used to play tennis, with a towel wound around his neck. Only he's bright, I mean bright in a stupid way, and the whole thing's absurd.

The telephone rang and rang until a cold, refined woman's voice, with a marked Roman accent, answered. "No, His Honour isn't home, he's at Strasbourg. What do you want?" "I'm a friend," I said, "an old friend. Can you tell me how to reach him? It's something very important." "I'm sorry," said the cold, refined voice, "His Honour's at a meeting. If you like you can leave a message and I'll get it to him as soon as

possible." I hung up and went back to the courtroom, but not
to the place where I'd been sitting. I stayed at the upper edge
of the semi-circular room, behind the *carabinieri*. At this
particular moment there was widespread murmuring. Leo
must have come out with one of his usual witticisms. His face
wore the malicious expression of someone who has pulled a
fast one. At the same time I detected a sad look. Federico, too,
as he shuffled the papers in front of him, seemed oppressed by
sadness, like a weight on his shoulders. I had an urge to cross
the courtroom, to stand in front of the judge's bench, amid
camera flashes, to say something to the two of them and grasp
their hands or something of the sort. But what could I say?
That it was a little misunderstanding that couldn't be corrected? Because just as I thought of this I realized that it was,
indeed, an enormous little misunderstanding that couldn't be
corrected, that the roles had been allotted and it was impossible not to play them. I had come with my notebook and pen,
hadn't I? Just looking at them play their parts I was playing
one of my own. I was to blame for falling in with the game,
because there's no escape and everyone of us is to blame in his
own way. All of a sudden I was overcome by weariness and
shame and, at the same time, I was struck by an idea I couldn't
decipher, a desire for Simplification. In a split second, in
pursuit of a dizzily unwinding skein, I realized that we were
there because of something called Complication, which for
hundreds and thousands and millions of years has piled up,
layer upon layer, increasingly complex circuits and systems,
forming us as we are and all that we live through. I longed for
Simplification, as if the millions of years which had produced
Federico, Leo, Maddalena, "Little Pol" and myself had magi-
cally faded out into a split second of vacant time and I could
imagine us, all of us, sitting on a leaf. Well, not exactly
sitting, because we had become microscopic in size, and
mononuclear, without sex, or history or reason, but with a
flicker of awareness which allowed us to recognize one

another, to know that we, we five, were there on a leaf, sucking up dewdrops as if we were sipping drinks at a table of the Caffè Goliardico, having no other function than to sit there while another kind of record player played another kind of *Dusty Road*, in a different form but with the same substance.

While I lingered, absorbed in my thoughts, on the leaf, the court rose, and so did the onlookers; only Leo remained seated in his cage and lit a cigarette. Perhaps it was a scheduled recess, I don't know, but I tiptoed outside. The air was clear and the sky blue; in front of the courthouse an ice-cream cart seemed to be abandoned, and few cars passed by. I started to walk towards the docks. On the canal a rusty barge, apparently without an engine, was gliding silently by. I passed near it, and aboard there were Leo and Federico, the one with his devil-may-care expression, the other grave and thoughtful. They were looking at me questioningly, obviously expecting an answer. And at the stern, as if she were holding the tiller, sat Maddalena, radiant with youth and smiling, like a girl aware of her youthful radiance. Do you remember *Dusty Road*? I wanted to ask them. But all three were static and motionless, and I realized that they were overly coloured, lifelike plaster figures, in the caricature poses of mannequins in a shop window. And so, of course, I said nothing but merely waved as the barge carried them away. Then I walked on, towards the docks, with slow, cadenced steps, trying not to tread on the cracks in the pavement, the way, as a child, I tried in a naive ritual to regulate by the symmetry of stones my childish interpretation of a world as yet without scansion or meter.

WAITING FOR WINTER

Then the smell of all those flowers . . . positively nauseating. The house, too, the rain veiling the trees, the objects in glass cases—Spanish fans, a pregnant Madonna of Cuzco, baroque angels, seventeenth-century pistols—all of them nauseating. This, too, was sorrow, one of its signs of pain—the sheer unbearableness of the things around us, their stolid, peremptory presence, impervious to change, living in unassailable immanence, unassailable because of its flagrant and innocent physical presence. I shan't make it, she said to herself; I know I shan't make it. As she spoke, she touched her warm forehead and braced herself against the back of the chair. She felt a knot of grief in her throat, and she looked in the mirror. She saw a noble, austere, almost haughty figure and thought: That's me, it's not possible. But it *was* she and there, too, lay her pain. Part of the sorrow of an old woman, wounded by death, was the pain already inherent in that figure of a pale, well-dressed old lady, her head covered by a black lace mantilla, a mantilla made with weary skill, as she well remembered, in a dark room, by taciturn and unhappy Spanish women. And she thought of Seville, many years before, the Giralda Tower, the Virgin of the Macarena, the solemn commemoration, in a hall with sober dark furniture, of a long-dead poet.

At this moment there was a knock at the door, and Françoise appeared. "Madame, the Minister is asking if you will see him." What a treasure, Françoise! She seemed so tiny, so frail, with her mouselike face and the round glasses which made her look like an ageless child; she was so totally and obtusely intelligent. "Tell him to wait in the small drawing room," she answered. "I'll be there in a few moments." She liked to talk this way. "A few moments," "a second," "let him wait a moment"—these gave her an urbane way of being proud and detached from herself, like an actor who wants to be a different person on stage in order to forget the emptiness he feels within. She looked again into the mirror and adjusted the mantilla. You mustn't cry, she said to the beautiful old woman looking out at her. Remember, you mustn't cry.

But she couldn't have cried. Because the Minister was pink-cheeked, pudgy and dressed in black; he bowed and kissed her hand; he was a man who was equal to the situation; he was cultivated, unlike most of his kind, and sincerely admired the dead writer. These things didn't call for tears. If he had been a mediocre, indifferent governmental type, carrying out his official duty, uttering appropriate set phrases and ceremonial commonplaces, then she might have given way to her diffuse and ambiguous sorrow. But not with the man who stood before her, genuinely regretful for the loss to the nation. "Our culture," he said, "has lost its greatest voice." This was incontrovertibly true, but it left no room for tears. She thanked him with a clear, honest sentence. This, too, belonged to the man-made conventional code of mourning, which has no connection with the dark shapes of sorrow. How she would have liked to cry! Then he struck a note of gratitude, a feeling less intense than sorrow, one which, for the moment, lay at the outer edge of her mind, together with nostalgia. And, with that gratitude, he spoke of plans and projects, of a debt of appreciation, which the government wanted to repay with a museum or a foundation, giving grants and fellowships and official celebrations. Recurrent celebrations, he specified. This brightened her, brought her a comfortless relief, causing her to think of a future that had already arrived, of a conventional monument. She reflected, also, how the nation had grown, matured and turned intelligent, in its fashion, something that he had hoped for all his life. Yes, she said, yes, certainly the nation deserved this inheritance. She thanked the Minister for the proposal and the offer, but she was still living in this house and here, for a short time, she would stay. Life can last only so long, and she didn't want to share hers with a nation's feelings, however noble.

Meanwhile the sun had risen higher, and a crowd had gathered in the garden. The Minister took his leave, and she went to stand at the window. The rain had given way to watery mist, which seemed to rise out of the ground. Cars drew up silently, and out of them got solemn-faced men whom the master-of ceremonies met with an umbrella and led to the door. The functional and efficient formality of a state funeral afforded her subtle relief because it appealed to her pragmatic sense of ritual. She realized that she could not linger in her solitude, and so she drew the curtains and started down the stairs, without holding on to the banister, slowly, her head held proudly high, her eyes dry, looking people in the eye as if she saw nobody, as if her look were trained elsewhere, perhaps towards the past or into herself, but certainly not there, among the objects of the tastefully arranged vigil room. She took her place at the head of the coffin, as if she were watching over a living man rather than a dead one, waiting for people to bow, kiss her hand and murmur words of sympathy and farewell. And while she stood there, removed from herself as well as from others, her heart beat calmly and regularly, remaining apart from the absolute devastation that was like a physical weight on her shoulders, from the terrible, incontrovertible evidence of the facts.

She let Françoise break in on the line, greeting her with serene detachment as if she were another visitor. Submissively, almost with relief, she let herself be led down what seemed an endlessly long hall and drank a hot broth, which was like yet another obligation imposed upon her. "No, I don't want to rest," she said in response to the girl's affectionate solicitude. "I'm not tired, and you needn't worry about me. I'll bear up." The words came from far away, as if someone else were pronouncing them, and she let Francoise oblige her to lie down, unlacing her shoes and passing a handkerchief dipped in eau de cologne across her forehead. He was running on the beach; behind the beach were the ruins of a Greek temple, and he was stark naked, nude like a Greek god with a laurel crown on his head. His testicles danced in a comical way as he ran, and she couldn't help laughing. She laughed so hard that she thought she was choking, and then she woke up.

She woke up abruptly, with a feeling of anxiety because she must have slept too long and everything must be over; visits, speeches, ceremonies, the funeral, perhaps even the day. Now it must be evening; Françoise was surely waiting in the hall, with reddened eyes and the air of a stoic sparrow, waiting to tell her: "I had to let you sleep. You couldn't hold out any longer." She went to the door, where she could hear the murmur of the guests below. From the anteroom she heard the Chinese clock strike two frivolous strokes. All of a sudden and for the first time, she hated that tiny, precious, monstrous timepiece. And yet she had bought it herself, imagining that she'd always treasure it. No, she said to herself forcefully, I won't think of Macao. For today I don't want to remember anything. In fact, she had slept for only ten minutes. She went into the bathroom and redid her make-up. The short sleep had disarranged her hair and left two deep furrows in the powder on her cheeks. She thought of masking their pallor with some rouge, then decided against it. She brushed her

teeth in order to dull the taste of camphor in her mouth.
Strange that the nausea brought on by so many flowers in the
house should take on the taste of camphor.

She went out, knowing that Françoise would be waiting in
the small drawing room. She had made an appointment with
the German publisher for two o'clock and didn't want to keep
him waiting. When she came in, the solemn gentleman stood
up and made a brief bow. He was stout, obese in fact, and
somehow this cheered her. Françoise was sitting down with a
notebook on her lap. "If you prefer to speak in your own
language, my secretary will serve as interpreter." The corpu-
lent gentleman nodded. He spared her banal outpourings and
came straight to the point, in honest, businesslike fashion, a
procedure that had its advantages. "I'm buying the diary," he
said in French. "Your husband lived in my country during
crucial years; he knew important political and literary people,
and his memoirs are valuable to us." He gave a slight cough
and fell silent, in anticipation of a response that was not
forthcoming. This seemed to perplex him because he stiffened
and advanced, boldly, into the area of money. "I'll pay in
marks," he said, "right away, before there's a contract; all I
need is an option." He spoke in German, and Françoise
promptly translated. The interposition of a translation made
the proposal less vulgar, and she was grateful to him for this
subtlety. Also it facilitated her reply; her words, passed on by
Françoise in other words that were to her incomprehensible,
took on a life of their own, which did not belong to her or
concern her, which no longer had a meaning. She would have
her secretary write to him, she said, but surely he understood
that this was no time for decisions. Of course she would take
into account that this was the first offer, but for the moment,
if he would excuse her, she must fulfil other obligations . . .
She looked to Françoise. Other obligations . . . she didn't
quite know which, and didn't care. Françoise was looking at
her notebook and taking care of everything. As she followed

Françoise, she gave in to this childish feeling. The sensation of being an abandoned child rose from the buried depths of her weary old body and broke through the ruins of the intervening years, giving her, once more, an overwhelming urge to sob and weep without restraint, and, at the same time, an almost feverish lightheartedness. For a moment she felt that the child reawakened within her might jump and dance or sing a nonsense song. Whatever had given her the urge to cry also took the urge away. And then a harsh light was coming out of the library, the floor was covered with wires, and someone was talking overloudly. "They're after an interview for the TV evening news," said Françoise. "The agency president called in person. I set a limit of three minutes, but if you don't feel up to it, I'll send them away. *Ils sont des bêtes*," she added scornfully.

It wasn't actually so. The TV reporter was an emaciated, intelligent-looking young man, tormenting the microphone with his bony hands. He seemed to be very well acquainted with the dead writer's work, and began by quoting from one of his youthful books. Beneath his acute but casual manner she felt a touch of embarrassment. He asked her to interpret a sentence which had become proverbial, symbolic of a whole generation, a sentence which even schoolbooks had picked up, in a positive sense, of course, because schoolbooks go for the positive. And here he was, asking her whether, in that definition of man, there wasn't a grain of irony, a perfidiously disguised negative hint. The insinuation made her feel happy. It allowed her to make an evasive reply, disguised as improvisation, to take refuge in the role of the great man's widow, who can reveal his taste in neckties. And so her answer was disarmingly banal, so inadquate that it lived up to exactly what the reporter expected. It confirmed, in the highest degree, that she was a subtly intelligent woman, the perfect helpmeet, who could provide precious first-hand information. All of which led, inevitably, to a biographical indiscretion, a subtle indiscretion, because the reporter was well-mannered and hoped, for the benefit of the TV audience, that she would tell him an episode of their life story. Which meant *his* life story. And she obliged—why not?—with a moralistic tale, one tinged with nobility, because that is what the public relishes, especially the everyday public. As she spoke, she had a feeling of bitterness towards herself. She would rather have told a quite different story, but not to this well-mannered young man, under the dazzling lights. She fell silent and smiled, in an exhausted but dignified manner.

Of the drive to the cathedral she registered nothing except for such confused fleeting images as the senses take in but do not retain. She was driven in a black car, upholstered in grey, with a muffled engine and a silent driver. At the service, too, she was there and not there, present with her body alone while she allowed her mind to range at random through the geography of memory: Paris, Capri, Taormina, and then, suddenly, a picturesque humble cottage which—it was almost funny—she couldn't place. She concentrated her efforts on a room whose insignificant details she vividly remembered, on a plain brass bed with a simple picture of the Holy Family hanging above it. Incredible that she couldn't recall the location. Where *was* it? Meanwhile the archbishop had pronounced a long homily, doubtless of a very high calibre. She felt cold. This, she thought, was the only sensation, indeed the only feeling that could hold her attention. Her stomach was cold, as if a huge block of ice were pressing against its walls, so that during the rest of the service she kept her hands tightly folded on her lap. Then the cold spread to her limbs, not into her hands, which were burning, but into her arms and shoulders, her legs and feet, which were without feeling, as if frozen, although she spasmodically wriggled her toes. Shivers ran through her body, and she couldn't hide them. She clenched her teeth so that they would not chatter, until she felt pain in the muscles of her face and neck. Françoise became aware that she was ill at ease; she took her hands into her own and whispered into her ear something which she did not catch, perhaps that she should leave. It didn't matter, because the ceremony was over, the coffin was being borne down the central aisle, and she found herself back in the same car with the same driver, who was taking her home, while Françoise had thrown her coat over her and put an arm around her shoulders in an attempt to warm her. It wasn't easy to part company graciously, to convey to Françoise, tactfully but firmly, that she didn't want her to stay overnight, that she wanted to enter and remain in the big, empty house unaccompanied, that the maid could attend to any need, that this was the first evening of her solitude and she wanted to enter into her solitude alone. Finally she drew herself away, Françoise kissed her, her eyes shining with tears, and she went into the silent front hall. Immediately she rang the bell for the maid and told her to withdraw because there was nothing to be done, except, please, to disconnect the telephone. As she went up the stairs she heard the odious Chinese clock strike seven times. She stopped on the landing and opened, almost greedily, its glass case, then deliberately advanced the minute hand to eight, nine, ten, eleven, twelve o'clock. When it reached there, she said to herself: It's already tomorrow. After that she went through another full cycle and said: It's already the day after tomorrow. Then she turned the hand the other way, and the clock obediently struck decreasing numbers. She went back down the stairs and into the library, where there was a vague smell of stale cigarettes. In order to drive it away, she lit a stick of incense and threw open a window. It was pouring rain. In the fireplace the maid had laid a little pyramid of logs, with pine cones for kindling. At the touch of a match flames shot up so brightly that there was no need for the hanging lamp. She turned it off. Then she opened the safe and took out a mahogany box. The manuscripts were piled up in perfect order, like banknotes, with rubber bands around them.

On every bundle there was a date, and the writer's signature.
She pulled them all out and looked them over. It was difficult
to choose. She thought of the novel, but decided against it.
The novel should come last, perhaps in February. And it was
too soon for the play. She paused over the other bundles. The
poems would be a good choice, but perhaps the diary would
be better still. She weighed it in her hand and looked at the
length. Three hundred was the number on the last page. Good
God! She sat down on the armchair in front of the fireplace
and crumpled the first page into a ball, so as to be able to
throw it into the fire without having to lean too far forward. It
turned a tobacco colour before turning to ashes. Poor fool, she
said, poor dear fool. She leaned back in the chair and looked
up at the ceiling. The winter would be long; it had scarcely
begun. She felt tears flood her eyes and let them run down her
cheeks, abundant, uncontrollable.

A RIDDLE

Last night I dreamed of Miriam. She was wearing a long white dress which, from a distance, seemed like a nightgown. She was walking along the beach; the waves were dangerously high and breaking in silence; it must have been the beach at Biarritz, but it was totally deserted. I was sitting on the first of an interminable line of empty deck chairs, but perhaps it was another beach because at Biarritz I don't remember deck chairs like those; it was just an imaginary beach. I waved to her, inviting her to sit down, but she went on walking, as if she didn't know me, looking straight ahead and, when she passed close by, I was struck by a gust of cold air, like an aura which she carried behind her: and then, with the unsurprised amazement of a dream, I realized that she was dead.

Sometimes it's only in a dream that we glimpse a plausible solution. Perhaps because reason is fearful; it can't fill in the gaps and achieve completeness, which is a form of simplicity; it prefers complexity, with all its gaps, and so the will entrusts the solution to dreams. But then tomorrow, or some other day, I'll dream that Miriam's alive, that she'll walk close to the sea, respond to my call and sit down on a deck chair belonging to the beach at Biarritz or to an imaginary beach. With her usual

19

languid, sensual gesture she'll push back her hair, look out to sea, point to a sailing boat or a cloud, and laugh. And we'll laugh together because here we are, we've made it, we've kept our appointment.

Life's an appointment—what I'm saying is very banal, Monsieur, I realize; the only thing is that we don't know when, where, how, and with whom. Then we think: if I'd said this instead of that or that instead of this, if I'd got up late instead of early, today I'd be imperceptibly different from what I am, and perhaps the world would be imperceptibly different, too. Or else it would be the same and I couldn't know it. For instance, I shouldn't be here telling a story, proposing a riddle that has no solution or else that has always had an inevitable solution, only I don't know about it and so, every now and then, rarely, when I'm having a drink with a friend, I say: Here's a riddle for you, let's see how you solve it. But then, why do you care about riddles? Do you go in for puzzles and the like, or is it just the sterile curiosity with which you observe other people's lives?

An appointment and a journey, this too is banal, I mean as a definition of life; it's been said any number of times, and then in the great journey there are other journeys, our insignificant trips over the crust of this planet, which is journeying also, but where to? It's all a riddle; perhaps you find me a bit odd. But, at that time, I had come to a standstill; I was stuck in a morass of boredom, in the lethargic mood of a man who is no longer very young, but not completely an adult, who is simply waiting for life.

And instead Miriam came on the scene. "I'm the Countess of Terrail, and I have to get to Biarritz." "And I'm the Marquis of Carabas, but I seldom leave my estate." That's exactly how it began, with this exchange. We were at Chez Albert, near the Porte Saint-Denis, not exactly a stamping ground for countesses. In the afternoon, after I'd closed the shop, I went to this bistrot for a drink. It's gone now and, in its place, there's one of those establishments that sell human flesh on film—it's the times. Albert would have liked to be buried at Père-Lachaise, because Proust is there, but I think he wound up in the cemetery at Ivry, another sign of the times. The old days—I don't mean to hark back to the past—but they were different, they really were. Take today's motor cars: the engine's all squeezed in—you could wrap it up in a handkerchief—and there's not even room to take the carburettor apart. Albert wasn't exactly my partner, but he might just as well have been because he got hold of many of the cars. He'd been a racing driver before there were macadam roads, when drivers wore special goggles to keep out the dust. He was a wee slip of a man, grown melancholy from standing behind the bar, who laughed only when he'd had a glass too many. At such moments he drew off some Alsatian beer and put a pitcher of it on the bar, just like in a cowboy film, exclaiming: "Speed!" Speed had done him in, but not too much; he was lame in one leg and his left hand had lost its grip. He was the one to get hold of the car that had belonged to Agostinelli, that is, to Proust. Lord knows how he did it. Agostinelli was Proust's chauffeur, and a good fellow; together they visited all the Gothic cathedrals of Normandy. I don't know if there was anything between them, and it doesn't really matter. Proust, as you know, had his particular tastes. Anyhow, to go back to what I was saying, during my first year of Literature at the university I'd written a paper that I thought I might turn into a thesis, but then I dropped out; the Sorbonne and its professors seemed pointless to me. My thesis was to be entitled *What Proust Saw from a Car*. Obviously the car, not Proust, was what interested me. One fine day I made up my mind and sold the piece for publication in two instalments in a third-class magazine, a feeble imitation of *Harper's Bazaar* (I'm not telling you the name, so you won't find it) and, God knows how, it fell into Albert's hands. He took that for granted; everything fell into his hands. And then, you know how life is, like a

woven fabric in which all the threads cross, and what I want
one day is to see the whole pattern. That's why, one evening, I
went to Chez Albert with a copy of the magazine under my
arm and ordered a drink. I was wandering about Saint-Denis
because I'd been told that, in the area, there was a body shop
owned by an old man who repaired vintage cars. I was a
proper mechanic, because I grew up in a garage at Meudon,
the town where Céline lived. Not that I knew him; he was a
bad egg, they say, but a good doctor, apparently, especially to
the poor. Albert saw the magazine under my arm. "There's a
piece in there about Proust's car," he said, "by a lunatic who
signs himself the Marquis of Carabas." "I'm the Marquis of
Carabas," I said, "but for the moment I'm what they call
fallen on hard times. I'm looking for the Pegasus body shop,
where I hear there's a job." Albert looked at me hard, as if to
see whether I was joking, but I wasn't; I was in low spirits.
"Don't take it so hard, my boy; the shop's in that courtyard
over there, and so is Agostinelli's car, which I brought in last
Sunday. I bought it at a junkyard in Suresnes, where they
didn't have the foggiest idea what it was. Now it's only a
matter of putting it back into working order."

And that's what we spent the summer doing. "This one's
not for sale," said Albert. "It's the car in which I want to run
my last race, destination Père-Lachaise, with a little band
behind, playing *En passant par la Lorraine.*" Lorraine is
where he came from, of course. I don't know if you can
visualize Proust's car, but probably you've seen a photograph
of it. It was a monument, with headlights like searchlights,
which served, on the trip through Normandy, to light up the
façades of the various cathedrals. When Proust and Agostinelli arrived in a town after dark, they drove through the
empty streets up to the cathedral square, stopping on a slight
incline so that the headlights would point upwards and illu-
minate the tympanum. "Agostinelli . . ." Proust would say,
and open the volume of Ruskin, which was his bible. This is

all true: he wrote it up in the *Le Figaro* of 1907 under the title *Impressions de route en automobile*. Of course, I was never quite sure that our car really had been Proust's. In the junk-yard where Albert had bought it there was no registration paper and it was impossible to trace the original owner. But, in the glove compartment, there was a pair of gloves, which Albert insisted were the real thing. If he liked the idea, what was wrong with it? Only the car wasn't used for his funeral; but that's another story.

When the owner of the repair shop died, I took over. For some time I had been a silent partner. Monsieur Gélin had given me a free hand and I had made a pile of money, partly thanks to Albert, who found the vintage cars. Sales were my affair; I created a mid-city headquarters for public relations because we couldn't receive prospective buyers at the shop. It was a microscopic but handsome set-up on the fashionable Avenue Foch: a waiting room and a panelled office with two leather-upholstered chairs and a brass plate on the door: PEGASUS. DE-LUXE VINTAGE CARS. I received customers twice a week—Saturday afternoon and Sunday morning—as adver-tised. Most of the time I was bored to death because there was seldom more than one buyer a month. But seven or eight sales a year yielded all the money I wanted. Albert managed to find old wrecks that cost him a song and he had made connections with a repair shop in Marseilles which sold us museum pieces for a pittance. All we had to do was fix them up, but that was quite a job. I enjoyed it, and I took on a bright, nimble-fingered young assistant, the son of one of Albert's cousins, called Jacob who, like him, came from Lorraine. For three or four years we restored a bit of everything: Delages, Aston Martins, a Hispano-Suiza, an Isotta Fraschini, and even a 1922 Fiat Mefistofele, the most beautiful racing car in the world. That one wasn't a car, really; it was a torpedo, a copy of the 1908 original, and in 1924 it set a world speed record. The customers were usually Americans, rolling in money,

mad about Europe, with an abominable accent and a craving
for vintage cars. They pictured themselves as so many Fitzger-
alds, geniuses and wastrels, drunk on champagne, Montmar-
tre, and *Sous le ciel de Paris.* Those, too, were the days. People
had been scared by bombs and the slaughter in the trenches
and they wanted to celebrate and feel themselves alive: let's
laugh and have fun; life's a gift to be enjoyed; we don't want
to be like the foolish virgins. There was an Egyptian, one of
our best customers, a jovial, fat fellow; he wanted a car every
three months, one for every season, he said, laughing like a
child. He drank like a sponge and wrecked the cars, one after
another. Eventually he came to a bad end; the French police
arrested him, I never knew why; for political reasons, they
said, but your guess is as good as mine. Albert wanted me to
get married. "Get yourself a wife, Carabas," he used to say.
"You're over thirty and you need the right kind of woman.
What's a man to do, in the house, after he's spent the day
fixing a hood? Time slips by, without our noticing, and you'll
be an old man before you know it." Albert was a bit of a
philosopher, like every good mechanic. You may not believe
it, Monsieur, but the study of automobiles is very instructive:
life's a gearbox, a wheel here, a pump there and then the
transmission, which links it all up and turns power into
movement, yes, just the way it is in life. Some day I'd like to
understand the workings of the transmission that ties the
components of my life together. It's the same idea; just open
up the hood and study the humming motor, then tie up all the
minutes, people, and events and say: here's the engine block
(that stage of my life); here's Albert (the starter); here am I (the
pistons with their valves) and here's the spark plug that sets
off the spark and gives the word to go. The spark was Miriam,
of course, as you probably realize, but what was the transmission? Not the obvious one, as I told Albert, which was a
Bugatti Royale, but the real, hidden one, which ties all the
components together and causes a car to move just the way

this one moved, with its rhythm, pulse, acceleration, speed and final slow-down.

"There's no resisting a Bugatti Royale," I said to Albert. "I'm going." He looked up from wiping the bar and I thought I saw a shadow of melancholy cross his eyes. "It'll give you problems," he said, "you know that better than I do, but I understand. It's your race. You've always been stuck between the starting line and the track and now you're in a position to run. You're too young and the fascination of risk is too strong."

But first I must go back, because that isn't where our conversation ended, I mean the conversation between Miriam and myself, when I told her I was the Marquis of Carabas but I had no mind to leave my estate. "Don't joke, please," she said. "I'm not joking," I replied. Then she repeated: "Don't joke, *please.*" And picking up her glass, distractedly, as if what she was about to say were the most natural thing in the world, "They want to kill me," she added. She said it with the voice of a woman who has seen, drunk, and loved too much and so was beyond lying. I stared at her, like a fool, not knowing what to answer and then I objected, ignobly, "What's in it for me?" She emptied her glass, hurriedly, with the melancholy smile of disillusionment. "Very little," she said; "you're quite right, practically nothing." She left some change on the table and wearily pushed back her hair. "Excuse me," she said, and went away. Besides her glass she had left a matchbox with Miriam written on it, and a telephone number. I didn't call; better pass it up, I said to myself. But the following Saturday, I met the Count. I was in my office on the Avenue Foch, summer was at hand and through the window I could see the new green leaves on the trees. I was reading a book by an Italian dandy who drove to Peking at the turn of the century— I don't remember his name—when the Count came in. Of course, I didn't know at first who he was. He was a stout man, no longer young, with a short reddish beard, wearing a navy-

blue blazer, light-coloured trousers, and old-fashioned sun-
glasses and carrying a newspaper and a cane, a rich banker or
lawyer type of fellow. He introduced himself and sat down,
crossing his legs awkwardly because of his weight. "I believe
my wife contacted you about a job proposal," he said deliberately, "and I'd like to clarify the terms." His tone of voice was
flat and bored, as if the matter did not concern him and he
wanted to get rid of it with a cheque. "We have an old car," he
went on, "a 1927 Bugatti Royale, and my wife has got it into
her head to take it to Biarritz, to take part in a rally at San
Sebastian." As I had foreseen, he pulled out a chequebook and
signed a cheque for an amount more than the price of the car.
His expression was more and more bored; as for me, I was
sparked up, but I tried to keep cool. There are plenty of drivers
around, I nearly said. If you put an ad in the paper there'll be
a flock of applicants; as for me, right now, I'm sorry, but I'm
very busy. Instead, he got in first: "I want you to turn down
my wife's offer." And he held out the cheque. It stayed in his
hand, because I was staring at him stupidly, taken by surprise.
At the same time I had a feeling that there was something
fishy about the whole story; it was too vague and contradic-
tory. I don't know why, perhaps just instinctively, I said: "I
don't know your wife or anything about a job proposal. I
don't know what you're talking about." It was his turn to be
taken aback, I was sure of it, but he didn't flinch. He tore up
the cheque and threw it into the wastepaper basket. "If that's
so," he said, "please excuse the interruption. My secretary
must have made a mistake; goodbye." As soon as he'd left, I
called the number Miriam had left me. The Hôtel de Paris
answered: "The Count and Countess have gone out. Do you
want to leave a message?" "Yes, it's a personal message for the
Countess; tell her that the Marquis de Carabas called, that's
all."

It was a genuine Bugatti Royale, a *coupé de ville*. I don't
know if that means anything to you, Monsieur; it's quite

understandable if it doesn't. Albert and I went to fetch it, in a little garage on the Quai d'Anjou, behind a wooden door opening onto a courtyard as musky as an English house, with the Seine running below. Albert couldn't believe his eyes. "It's impossible," he said, "impossible," caressing the long, tapering fenders; I don't know whether you get the idea, but the Bugatti has something of a woman's body about it, a woman lying on her back with her legs out in front of her. It was a superb specimen, the body in excellent condition, the damask velvet upholstery in fairly good shape aside from a few moth holes and a single tear. The main problem—at least at first sight—lay in the wheels and the exhaust pipes. The engine seemed unaffected by its long idleness and in need only of being roused from its slumber. We roused it successfully and drove it to the shop. The elephant on the hood was missing, and this was an unpleasant surprise, because you can't take a Bugatti Royale to a rally without its elephant. Perhaps you didn't know, but at the top of the radiator the Royale had a silver elephant sculpted by Ettore Bugatti's brother, Rembrandt. It wasn't just a trademark like the Rolls Royce's Spirit of Ecstasy or the Packard swan, it was a symbol, undecipherable, like all symbols; an elephant standing on his hind legs, with his trunk upraised and trumpeting, in a gesture of attack or mating. Is it too glib to say that these two go together? Perhaps so. But just imagine this: a Bugatti Royale on its haunches, climbing a slight incline, with fenders flared, ready to gather speed and intoxication, with power throbbing behind a fabulous radiator grille and, atop it, an elephant with upraised trunk.

I wanted to stay on the sidelines. Albert called the Countess at the Hôtel de Paris to find out if she knew what had become of the elephant. It had simply disappeared; in any case, it was lost, he reported. The car had been standing too long; she says to make a copy. And so we had three weeks to do something about it, while we were touching up the engine and the

upholstery. One cylinder needed adjusting, but that was not a
big job. The upholsterer was a wily young fellow with a shop
on the Rue Le Peletier, who sent antique fabrics to be repaired
by the nuns of a certain convent. There's nobody like a nun
for a painstaking job, believe me, and their mending was
invisible; it was all done on the reverse side, where it left a
network of threads like a telephone exchange. The worst
thing was the elephant. A sculptor of sorts offered to make a
clay copy to be covered with metal, but bumps and jolts would
soon have caused it to crack. Finally Albert thought of a
cabinetmaker from Lorraine—this story is full of Lorrainers
—who had a shop in the Marais, an old fellow who carved
wood in naturalistic style. It was easy enough to find a photograph of the elephant, which we took to the old man, together
with the exact measurements, telling him to make an identical
copy. After that we had to see to the chrome plating, and that
came out satisfactorily. Of course, if you looked at the figure
when the car was standing still you could see that it was a
fake, but in motion it seemed like the real thing.

The morning of our departure was quite an event. Albert
had fallen completely into the role of father, and kept asking
whether I needed this or had forgotten that. The day before
I'd bought a leather suitcase—the car and the trip deserved
nothing less—as well as a cream-colored linen jacket and
another in leather and an Italian silk scarf. When I got to the
Hôtel de Paris a liveried doorman opened the car, and, feeling
like the Marquis of Carabas, I told him to call the Countess. A
porter came with a valise and a vanity case; she arrived, on her
husband's arm, greeted me distractedly and got into the back
seat. Here was the first surprise of the day. I had been fearful
of seeing the Count again because I didn't exactly like him,
but he spoke to me as if we'd never met, playing the part to
perfection. It was a Monday towards the end of June. "We'll
meet in Biarritz a week from today," he said affably to his
wife. "If you like you can send your driver to pick me up at the

station—my train gets in at eight thirty-five in the evening;
otherwise we'll meet at the Hôtel des Palais." I went into first
gear, and she gave a brief wave of her hand through the open
window.

The second surprise was her telling me to take the Route
Nationale 6, and her tone of voice, a dry, decisive tone which
seemed to reflect a strong will or else some sort of phobia. I
objected that this wasn't the shortest way to Biarritz. "I want
to take another route," she said sharply, "I'd appreciate it if
you didn't argue the point." And there was a third surprise as
well. When I first met her at Chez Albert she was so defenceless and such an open book that I thought I could read her
whole life on her face; now, instead, she had withdrawn
behind a mask of distance and reserve, like a real countess. She
was beautiful, and that was no surprise, but now she seemed
to me of an absolute beauty, because I understood that no
beauty in the world is greater than that of a woman, and this,
you'll understand, Monsieur, put me into a sort of frenzy.
Meanwhile the Bugatti glided over the gentle, inviting roads
of France, up and down and along level stretches, the way our
roads go, bordered by plane trees on either side. Behind me the
road retreated, before me it opened up, and I thought of my
life and the boredom of it, and of what Albert had said to me,
and I felt ashamed that I'd never known love. I don't mean
physical love, of course, I'd had that, but real love, the kind
that blazes up inside and breaks out and spins like a motor
while the wheels speed over the ground. It was like that, a sort
of remorse, an awareness of mediocrity or cowardice. Up to
now my wheels had turned slowly and tediously over a long,
long road, and I couldn't remember a single landscape along
the way. Now I was travelling another road, which led nowhere, with a beautiful and distant woman who was escaping
or fleeing from I knew not what. It was a useless race across
France, I felt quite sure, on a road as empty as those that had
gone before. Those were my exact thoughts at that particular

moment. Limoges was not far, we were deep in the country-side, where farmers were working among their fruit trees. Limoges, I thought, what does Limoges have to do with my life? I drew the car over to the side of the road and stopped. Turning towards her, I said: "Look here. . . ." Before I could say any more she laid a finger gently across my lips and murmured: "Don't be a fool, Carabas." Without another word she got out and came to sit beside me. "Go on," she said, "I know that we're taking an absurd route, but perhaps every-thing's absurd, and I have my reasons."

It's a curious sensation to arrive in a strange city, knowing that there you'll love with a love you've never experienced before. That's how it was. We stopped at a little hotel on the river—I don't remember the name of the river that runs by Limoges. The room had faded wallpaper and very ordinary furniture; in those years many hotels were like that; you've only to look at the films of Jean Gabin. Miriam asked me to say that she was my wife, she didn't want to identify herself and the hotel didn't ask for the papers of both members of a couple. From the room we could see the river, bordered by willows; it was a fine night and we fell asleep at dawn. "Who is it you're running away from, Miriam," I asked her. "What's wrong in your life?" But she laid a finger across my lips.

An absurd route, as I said before. We went down to Rodez and then towards Albi and its vineyards, because of a land-scape she wanted to see. I thought it was an outdoor view but it was a painting, and we found it. We skipped Toulouse and made for Pau, because her mother had spent her childhood there, and I lingered over the idea of her mother as a child, in a boarding school which we couldn't locate. It was the first time I'd thought of the childhood of a woman companion's mother, a new and strange sensation. We looked at the splen-did square and at the houses, with their white attic windows suspended from tile roofs, and I imagined a winter in Pau, behind one of those windows. I was tempted to say: Listen,

Miriam, let's forget about everything else and spend the winter behind one of these windows, in this city where nobody knows us.

When we got to Biarritz it was Saturday; the rally was to be the next day. I thought we'd go to the Hôtel des Palais and take two rooms there, but she chose to go elsewhere, to the Hôtel d'Angleterre, and she signed the register in my name. In luxury hotels, too, they don't ask to see a woman's papers. She was hiding out, obviously, and I was haunted by the strange sentence she had pronounced on the day of our first meeting, a subject to which she refused to return. I put my hands on her shoulders and looked into her eyes—we had gone down to the beach at sunset, seagulls were standing around, a sign of bad weather, they say, and some children were playing in the sand. "I want to know," I told her, and she said: "Tomorrow you'll know everything. Tomorrow evening, after the rally, we'll meet here on the beach and go for a drive in the car. Don't insist, please."

The rally rules demanded that every driver be dressed in the style of the period of his car. I had bought a pair of baggy Zouave-style trousers and a tan cloth cap with a visor. "This is a show," I said to Miriam; "it's not a race, it's a fashion parade." But she said no, I'd see. Competition wasn't the order of the day, but almost. The course ran along the ocean, a road riddled with curves hanging over the water: Bidart, Saint-Jean-de-Luz, Donibane and, finally, San Sebastian. We set out three by three, our names drawn by lot, regardless of the type of car. The time was to be clocked and calculated according to each car's horsepower. And so we started out with a 1928 Hispano-Suiza, called La Boulogne, and a bright red 1922 Lambda, a superb creation (suffice it to say that Mussolini had one). Not that the Hispano-Suiza was to be sneezed at; it was definitely elegant, with its bottle-green coupé body and long chrome hood. We were among the first to take off, at ten o'clock in the morning. It was a fine typically Atlantic day, with a cool breeze and clouds flitting across the sun. The Hispano-Suiza took off like a shot. "We'll let it go," I said to Miriam; "I refuse to let others set the pace; we'll catch up when I feel like it." The Lambda stayed quietly behind. It was driven by a fellow with a black moustache, accompanied by a young girl, probably rich Italians, who smiled at us and every now and then called out *ciao*. They remained behind us on all the curves until Saint-Jean-de-Luz, then they passed us at Hendaye, the border town, and began to slow up on the straight, flat road to Donibane. I thought it was strange that they should linger at this particular point. We had passed the Hispano-Suiza before arriving at Irun; now I meant to step on the accelerator and I expected the driver of the Lambda to do likewise. Instead, he let us pass with the greatest of ease. For a hundred yards or so we were side by side; the girl waved and laughed. "They're out for a good time," I said to Miriam. They caught up with us at the end of the straight, at which point there were two nasty curves in rapid succession. We'd tried them out the evening before, and they were imprinted on my memory. Miriam cried out when she saw them coming at us, pushing us towards the precipice. Instinctively I braked and then accelerated, managing to hit the Lambda. It was a hard, quick blow, enough to throw the Lambda off the road, to the left, where it slithered along the inside embankment for about twenty yards. I was following the scene in the rear-view mirror as the Lambda lost a fender against a pole, skidded towards the centre of the road and then back to the left where, having run out of all impetus, it bogged down in a pile of dirt. Plainly the passengers were not injured. I was drenched with cold sweat. Miriam clasped my arm. "Don't stay," she said, "please, please don't stay," and I drove on. San Sebastian was directly below us; no one had witnessed the incident. After passing the finish line I made for the improvised, open-air garage, but I didn't get out of the car. "It was intentional," I said; "they did it on purpose." Miriam was very pale, and speechless, as if petrified. "I'm going to the police to report it," I said. "Please," she murmured. "But don't you see that they did it on purpose?" I shouted. "That they were trying to kill us?" She looked at me, with an expression half troubled, half imploring. "You can take care of the car," I said; "get the bumper straightened while I walk around." And I got out, slamming the door; there was nothing seriously wrong with the car and the whole thing could have been just a bad dream. I wandered around San Sebastian, especially along the sea. It's a fine city, with those white late nineteenth-century buildings. Then I went into an enormous café—the sort you find only in Spain, the walls lined with mirrors and a restaurant attached to it—and ate some fried fish.

Miriam was waiting in the car, near the garage. She had put on make-up and regained her composure and the fear was gone. Mechanics straightened the bumper, the rally was over and people were streaming away. I asked her if we'd won anything. "I don't know," she answered, "it doesn't matter, let's go back to the hotel." I didn't notice the time; it must have been around three. As far as Irun we didn't say a word. At the border, when they saw that we'd taken part in the rally they waved us by, and we were back in France. It was only then that I noticed. I noticed by pure chance, because we had the sun at our backs and its reflection on the radiator ornament bothered me, as if it were sparkling in a mirror. Coming the other way, that morning, it hadn't been a bother because the wood had to some extent absorbed the chrome, leaving it opaque. I stopped the car, but I didn't get out and look more closely because I already knew. "They've changed the elephant," I said. "This one is in metal, steel or silver, I don't know which, but it's not the same." Then I thought of something else, something absurd, but I voiced it: "I want to see what's inside." Miriam looked at me and paled. Once more she was ashen grey, as at the time of the incident, and seemed to be trembling. "I'll tell you about it this evening," she said; "please, my husband will be here in a few hours and I want to go." "Is he the one you're afraid of?" I asked. "When I first met you, you told me something, do you remember? Is he the one?" She squeezed my hand, trembling. "Let's go, please," she said, "don't let's waste any more time. I want to go back to the hotel."

We made love intensely, almost convulsively, as if it were a last act, dictated by an impulse of survival. I lay, dazed, between the sheets, without sleeping, in the sort of drowsy state that allows the mind to wander from image to image. Before my eyes there paraded Albert and the Pegasus body shop, the attic on the square in Pau, a small metal elephant, a ribbon-like road along a cliff overhanging the ocean, with Miriam standing at the edge of the precipice until the Count noise-lessly crept up on her and pushed her over, and she fell, hugging the handbag which she never let go. That's how my mind was working when Miriam got up and went into the bathroom. My right arm travelled down the side of the bed to the floor, searching for the bag, my hand delicately opened it and felt the butt of a revolver. Unconsciously I took it, got quickly out of bed and dressed. I looked at my watch; there was plenty of time. When Miriam came out of the bathroom she grasped the situation but did not object. I told her to pack and wait for me. "No," she said, "I'll wait for you on the beach; I'm afraid to stay alone in a hotel room." "At half-past nine," I said. "Leave the car with me," she said; "it's wiser for you to go in a taxi." I went down to pay the bill and caught a cab. Mist was falling. I got out near the station and wandered about, wondering what I was going to do and knowing per-fectly well that I hadn't the slightest notion. It seemed per-fectly ridiculous to wait for a man I'd seen twice in my life, and what for? To threaten him, to say that I knew he meant to kill his wife? And what if he wouldn't give up the idea? What would I do if he reacted? I turned the little toylike revolver over and over in my pocket. There were a few people in the station, the loudspeaker announced the arrival of the train and I hid, trying to look casual, behind a column on the platform. After all, he already knew me. Shall I face up to him there, I wondered, or follow him along the street? The hand gripping the revolver was sweaty. At this point people began getting off the train: a group of carefree Spaniards, a nurse-maid with two blond children, a newly-wed couple, a few tourists. Finally the railway attendants opened all the train doors and, armed with brooms and suction pumps, began to clean up. A few seconds went by before I realized that he hadn't been on the train at all. Suddenly I was stricken with panic; not exactly panic but tremendous anxiety. I raced through the station, hailed a taxi, and made for the Hôtel des Palais. I could have gone on foot, but I was in a hurry. The hotel was magnificent, one of the oldest in the city, a majestic yet airy white structure. The receptionist examined the regis-ter from start to finish and from finish to start, running his finger down the list of guests. "No," he said, "we've no guest by that name." "Perhaps he hasn't arrived yet; look at the reservations, will you?" He took his list and examined it with the same care. "No, sir, I'm sorry, but there's nothing." I asked for the telephone and called the Hôtel d'Angleterre. "The lady left shortly after you," said the desk clerk. "Are you sure?" "Yes, she handed in the key and went off in the car; the porter loaded the luggage." I left the Hôtel des Palais and walked to the beach, which was only a few steps away. I went down the steps and walked slowly over the sand. It was half-past nine, a mist had fallen and the waves were high; summer nights at Biarritz can be chilly. At the place where we were to meet there was a bathhouse with a row of deck chairs. I sat down on one and looked out to sea. I heard a church bell ring out ten o'clock, then eleven and twelve. The revolver was still in my pocket; I was tempted to throw it into the ocean, but I couldn't do it, I don't know why.

Do you know, once I put an advertisement in *Le Figaro*: "Lost elephant looking for 1927 Bugatti." That's a good one, isn't it? But you've made me drink too much, Monsieur, although when it comes to drinking you're good company. Sometimes, when you've drunk a bit, reality is simplified; the gaps between one thing and another are closed, everything hangs together and you say to yourself: I've got it. Just like a dream.

But why are you interested in other people's stories? You too must be unable to fill in the gaps. Can't you be satisfied with your own dreams?

SPELLS

For instance, you see, these are my father's feet; I call them Constantine Dragases, like the last emperor of Byzantium, a brave and unfortunate men—they all betrayed him and he died along on the battlements—but you see them as two ordinary feet made of plastic. I found them on the beach last week; sometimes the sea washes pieces of dolls ashore. Well, I found these two legs and immediately I understood that it was Papa, from wherever he was, sending me a facsimile of his feet in order to meet my memories halfway. I *felt* it; I don't know if you understand.

And I said, well, yes, of course I understood, but couldn't we play at something else, outdoors, in the garden? In the house everyone was sleeping; it was an adventure to slip out while they were all taking their afternoon naps and the house was immersed in silence. But if that didn't suit her we could stretch out, flat on our stomachs, on the rug in her room and read *The Phantom of the Opera*. This time I wouldn't budge, I promised, so as not to disturb her reading. I revelled in it, I thought I was dreaming, when she read aloud, in a whisper, close to my ear. I'll be your humble listener, Cleliuccia, I said, I swear it. Then I wanted to kick myself because I'd blown it. Damn the carelessness that was always causing me to mix up Cleliuccia with the unhappy witch Melusina!

She threw me a fierce look through her one good eye and then took off the ridiculous glasses with one cardboard lens, letting her defective eye roll around in peace instead of rotating wildly as it did when she was angry. Words counted a lot for Melusina, how many times did she have to tell me so? Because words are *things*, of course, no need to repeat it, I got the idea: they were things transformed into the ghost of pure sound, and with the things of this world you have to be very careful, because they are sensitive, quite so. But how to make the point that her squint wouldn't be offended if she simply called it a squint instead of a lack of focus in the left eye? It wasn't even noticeable unless she was nervous, and she had long blond hair, and I liked her, even her ineptness at sports didn't bother me; I should have liked to tell her all these things. But it would have been disastrous to speak of her ineptness at sports after the unpardonable mistake of calling her Cleliuccia. Cleliuccia indeed! That was what Aunt Esther called her and for this reason she came close to hating my aunt, that is, if she hadn't been Aunt Esther, and you couldn't hate Aunt Esther, no matter how hard you tried. How *can* you hate someone like my mother, Clelia would ask, as if seeking my assent. True, very true, I answered with a feeling of relief; nobody can hate Aunt Esther because she's too good. Stupid, that's what she is, she retorted, and you can't hate somebody stupid; what I hate is clever people, clever and tricky. I knew whom she meant and preferred to change the subject. Not that it bothered me, perhaps I simply wasn't interested; I preferred playing in the garden. I was only three years younger and my company wasn't to be scorned. And then do you think it's good for you to stay in the house all day, in semi-darkness, among the dolls? I asked her. Didn't the doctor prescribe fresh air and sports? I looked out of the window and felt an enormous, almost overpowering urge to make for the pine woods. I was thinking of previous summers, and how things would never be the same. I could no longer count on the gateman's

son; during the year he had grown tall, there was a thin line of
hair under his nose, he smoked, stealthily, behind the garage,
and rode along the shore on a bicycle. He was called Ermanno
now and wouldn't have played Lothair to her Mandrake; I
wouldn't dare suggest it. Within a short time everything had
changed. What "everything", and why? I thought of the time
when Clelia was Diana, betrothed to the Man in the Iron
Mask, or the terrible Queen Maona, the snake charmer, and
Ermanno and I tried to discover the secret of her elixirs. Now
it seemed almost ridiculous, and so it must seem to her, too, as
she sat in her half-dark room, reading Gaston Leroux, Arsène
Lupin, and *The Dead Woman's Kiss*. Our races to the pine
woods and among the bushes . . . all gone, I knew it. Now, at
best, there was the walk to the beach, two boring hours under
the beach umbrella and, on Saturday evenings, ice cream at
one of the tables set out at the café of the Andrea Doria
Bathhouse. Then the same thing all over, day after day; only
ten days had gone by and the summer would never end. I
thought, first, of writing to my father, but what excuse was
there for asking him to come and take me away, just that I no
longer liked being there? And what Clelia had told me about
her new father, could I tell him that? No, I couldn't, I'd sworn
not to. I had to call him Uncle Tullio and be nice to him as he
was nice to me. When he arrived, on Saturdays, he always
brought two parcels, one for Clelia and one for me. In Clelia's
there was a doll, because she had a collection of dolls, even if
she no longer played with them. And what did I have to say?
Actually I liked Uncle Tullio; he was the jolliest fellow and,
when he was there, the house was no longer a morgue. On
Saturday evenings, he took us to the Andrea Doria Café, and I
could have two ice creams, including "Nero's Cup", with the
candied cherries. I liked the way he dressed, too, impeccably,
with a linen jacket and a bow tie. He and Aunt Esther made a
very fine couple; when we strolled on the promenade people
turned around to look at them and I was happy on my aunt's

behalf. My sister couldn't stay a widow for the rest of her life, said my mother; she did well to make a new life for herself, poor dear. Anyone would have said the same thing, to see her strolling on the promenade, in her pretty blue dress, her hair cut as short as a girl's, a happy woman on the arm of a husband who had forgotten the horrors of the War. Everybody seemed to have forgotten the War; they were all disporting themselves on the beach. As for me, I had no memory at all of the War; during the bombing I was in the process of being born. But from inside the house Aunt Esther's life didn't seem so happy, and I was in a position to know. On the day of my arrival she'd called me into the small drawing room with the spinet piano (why there, as if I were an honoured guest?) and almost implored me to have a good time this summer, such a good time. Play, play, my boy, to your heart's content! A strange request, since I'd come, just as in the preceding summers, looking for a good time. And why did she wring her hands? Be good to Cleliuccia, please; keep her company and play with her, do you hear? And she hurried out of the room as if she were about to cry.

To play with Cleliuccia . . . it was all very easy to say. And it would have been easy enough during the unusual days that followed, after the wind from the African desert had damaged the roof, carrying sand even into the drawing room, through the hole made by a flower pot which had rolled against the glass door onto the terrace. But one day it was *The Mystery of the Yellow Room* and another *Carmilla, Queen of the Witches' Sabbath*, and all those dolls lined up on the bookshelves and the half-dark room . . . I didn't know what games to suggest; my stock was exhausted. Aunt Esther's eyes were always shiny, and she had a vaguely absent air. After lunch she went to her room and stayed there the whole afternoon until she came out, wandered desolately about the house, and finally sat down at the spinet and stumbled through Chopin's *Polonaises*. I could only tiptoe from one room to another,

trying to think up something to do and keeping out of range
of the severe eyes of Flora, who would have looked at me
reproachfully because my aunt needed to rest and I was doing
everything possible to disturb her: Why didn't I go and snatch
a breath of fresh air in the garden?

It was a revelation. Anything else I could have imagined,
but not that. At first I couldn't believe it but on second
thoughts it was quite credible: I remembered how my Aunt
Esther had been two years before, a witty, energetic woman.
She used to take Clelia and myself to the beach on the luggage
rack of her bicycle, arriving hot and red in the face, with her
eyes gleaming and, in a second she was out of the cabin, in her
bathing suit and into the water, where she swam like a fish.
Something important and incredible must have happened to
reduce her to this condition. *This* is what happened, said
Clelia; did I understand? I understood, yes, but who had done
it? Clelia's eye rolled wildly, a sign of extreme nervousness,
but her mouth remained shut, as if she were afraid to pro-
nounce the name. Never mind; I understood. And *bewitched*
wasn't the word; better *possessed*, since the sorcery was the
work of a diabolical being. I could almost have laughed at the
idea of Uncle Tullio as Satan, with his bow tie and pomaded
hair, his formal and considerate ways. I felt sure, if she wanted
to know a secret, that my father thought he was ridiculous.
Well then, if that was the way I saw it, did I want her to tell me
the whole truth, did I want to know what this fellow with the
pomaded hair and the diabolical smile had been capable of
doing? That handsome Tullio with his bow tie had killed her
father, yes he had; he was at the root of all the trouble. No, he
hadn't exactly killed him with his own hands, of course, but it
came to the same thing. He'd turned him in to the Germans,
and she had proof, in the form of a certain letter, of which
she'd make a copy to show me. And why, did I know why?
Simply in order to cast a spell over that stupid mother of hers,
to possess her money and her life, that was why. This seemed

to me exaggerated, unthinkable, but I didn't argue about it, because Aunt Esther had told me not to contradict Clelia; it was bad for her health and brought on an attack. But that night I couldn't sleep. I dreamed of Uncle Tullio, wearing a trench coat, in command of a firing squad, with his bow tie sticking out from the trench coat collar. The man sentenced to death was Uncle Andrea, whom I had never known and whom I couldn't see because he was too far away, standing with his back to the wall. I knew he was Uncle Andrea because he called out: I'm Clelia's daddy! That cry woke me up in the middle of the night; the garden was full of crickets and the beach was empty. I stayed awake, listening to the roar of the sea for I don't know how long, perhaps until daybreak. But in the morning everything was just as usual, and the idea of writing to my father seemed absurd. The house was so beautiful, so bright, Aunt Esther had suggested that I go with her to do the weekend shopping, Clelia was working with wax and Uncle Tullio would be arriving the next day. He'd take us to the café and on Sunday evening we might go to see *Son of Tarzan* at the open-air cinema. Besides, a promise is a promise and I'd promised Clelia loyalty and silence.

Uncle Tullio arrived with a kitten, a black kitten with a white spot on its forehead, which I found adorable. The kitten was in a cloth-lined straw basket, a tiny creature that had to be fed milk with a spoon. He had a pink ribbon around his neck, and his name was Cece. He was a present for Clelia; perhaps he'll distract her a bit, there's no harm in trying, I heard Uncle Tullio say to Aunt Esther. I remember the forced smile on Clelia's face as she came down the stairs, the alarmed glance that she shot me and a rapid gesture, which I detected but could not decipher, but which seemed to say: Don't worry, don't be afraid. But afraid of what? And I remember the equally forced or, rather, fearful smile of Aunt Esther, who was worried lest Clelia fail to like the kitten and say so. Instead, she said he was a darling, a ball of fur. She thanked

Uncle Tullio with casual grace, but distractedly. She wasn't feeling up to scratch, she said, and she was busy finishing a wax puppet. For the time being Flora could look after the kitten. Cats are always happy in the kitchen; there's no place they like better. Later on, in her room, I found out why, and I couldn't stomach it. I'd had enough of such talk, honestly I had, and perhaps I'd better write to ask my father to take me away. And why did she insist on frightening me? It seemed as if she got a kick out of it. Just at that moment Flora cried out from downstairs, with a cry as penetrating as a drill, and then a lament, an invocation, tears and sobs like those of a death rattle. Clelia grasped and squeezed my hand. Oh, my God, she said, and then some incomprehensible words, followed by strange gestures. I realized that something terrible was going on, something mysteriously terrible and revolting. Clelia took off her glasses and laid them on the bed, as if she were afraid of breaking them, and her left eye rolled around wilder than I'd ever seen it. I felt fear rising within me like a fever. She had turned deadly pale; she clenched her fists and then her mouth stiffened, showing her teeth as if in a grin. She fell backwards and lay stiffly on the floor, twitching as if from an electric current. I ran, almost tumbling, down the stairs. I remember my disastrous entrance into the kitchen, where I nearly broke my neck by slipping on a spreading drop of oil which I failed to see. I remember Aunt Esther and Uncle Tullio trying to pull off Flora's stockings as she sat, moaning, on a chair. I remember the horror of seeing the stockings peeled off, taking with them strips of flesh and leaving brown spots on the legs. I remember my stammering phrases, the inability to express myself, the nausea in my mouth until I managed to summon up the breath to shout that Clelia was dying, after which I broke into tears.

The next day was one of silence. Clelia looked at me calmly, as if nothing had happened, as if the preceding evening she had not been at death's door. Sunlight poured into her room

through the wide-open window; it was late in the morning
and the house seemed flooded with suspense. Did I understand that the horrible thing which had happened to Flora
was intended for Clelia? Did I really feel, now, that I should
get away? Was I capable of writing to my father and leaving
them there, in that house? Would I really do it?

The day dragged on. We ate a bite of lunch, very late,
because Aunt Esther and Uncle Tullio spent the morning at
the hospital and then came back, bringing Flora with them,
her legs swathed in bandages after being treated for second-
degree burns. Of course there was no mention of *Son of
Tarzan*. Who could have wanted to see it? In the late afternoon
Uncle Tullio went back to the city and life resumed its normal
course, with the difference that we had to be on guard, intensely on guard, because danger hung over us and it might be
necessary to do something in a hurry. But why did danger
hang over us, that's what I wanted to know, and why was I
included; I had nothing to do with it, the problem was all
Clelia's. And what was the *something* that might have to be
done in a hurry? My heart was pounding. Dusk was falling
and the crickets were chirping madly. One of them must have
been on the windowsill, and it filled the room with sound. I
looked at Clelia's dolls, lined up on the shelves. I didn't like
those dolls, there was something wicked and threatening
about them, and I didn't want to look into the suitcase guard-
edly pulled halfway out from under the bed. I'd have preferred
to go away, yes, really, please, Melusina. The cricket fell
suddenly silent, and its silence underlined the silence of the
house, the garden, and the quiet evening. Something had to
be done at once, surely I understood, the treacherous mecha-
nism had been set in motion; it had hit Flora, but Flora wasn't
the real target, she knew it, and so did I; yes, look, silly boy, I
made this puppet out of wax, last night; don't gape like an
idiot, it's only a little animal; do you think it looks like the
real thing? And then she gave a little laugh when I cried out

the name. Cece, my eye! Silly! The cat he gave me isn't Cece, that's the name he gave him to fool simpletons like you. Now I'll tell you his real name, Matagot, yes that's it; don't stare at me as if I were mad, I can't stand it. I know the name means nothing to you, but that doesn't matter because I'm not fooled. You don't know about Matagot, only a few of us do; he's Beelzebub's cat, they are always together, the cat walking ten feet ahead of him on the left side, in order to prepare the spell for his master. Give me that paper cutter. She looked at the lovely creature as if it had the plague, and yet she had fashioned it herself, and very successfully; it was the spitting image of Cece, but I simply couldn't understand. A spell hung over us, certainly, yes, you little fool, over you, too, standing there as stiff as a scarecrow. Careful not to touch the victim with your hands, only with the instrument, and you must hold him up. Only stop calling him Cece or you'll ruin everything. Try to concentrate and repeat, silently: *Dies, mies, jasquet, benedo, efet, sovema enitemaus.* She struck him, sideways, with the paper cutter, and the head came off cleanly, without the wax crumbling; there were only a few white cracks like those on a piece of glass struck by a stone. Clelia took the white cloth off her head and blew out the candle, but I hadn't repeated the words. We'll see tomorrow, she said; the spell is cast.

That's how the game began, as if we were in the book about the witch Carmilla. Finally I too had something to do; I wouldn't spend the day hanging about the drawing room. But the day wasn't as exciting as I'd imagined. My only job was not to let Cece out of my sight for a single second. Perhaps I was the emissary of the priestess Melusina and he was the diabolical Matigot, but he was still a cat and behaved like one, like a stupid household cat, with no mystery about him. He spent part of the morning dozing in his basket, which obliged me to go repeatedly into the kitchen or to linger nearby, arousing the suspicion of that idiotic Flora, who saw me as a

threat to her jellies and jams, as if I could possibly go for the
sticky concoctions she guarded so jealously in the pantry.
Towards noon, Cece deigned to come out of the basket. Flora
had given him some milk in a bowl—obviously she held no
grudge against him for what had happened—and he licked
the edge of the bowl indifferently, like a spoiled child. Then
he continued to act like a cat, not in the least diabolically,
rolling onto his back and pawing the air as if to catch something to a cat's taste. Clelia had promised to take my place,
briefly, before lunch, but she didn't keep her word and I
resigned myself to waiting, seated on the small sofa in the
entrance hall and pretending to read the *Children's Encyclo-
paedia* while I kept an eye on the kitchen door. Finally Flora
called out that lunch was ready. Aunt Esther came in from the
garden with some geraniums which she put into a vase on the
console table in the entrance hall. The bell on the upstairs
floor echoed, with its metallic ring, in the kitchen. I guessed,
of course, what it meant and so did Aunt Esther and, sure
enough, Flora came back down with a dark look on her face.
Signorina Clelia didn't feel well and preferred to have lunch
in her room. Aunt Esther bowed her head over her plate and
sighed, and I laid my napkin on my knees. Lunch was silent,
as usual. There were ham and melon, and the melon was so
sweet that I'd gladly have had a second helping, while Aunt
Esther ate her portion listlessly; she had cut it up into tiny
squares and carried them to her mouth in an incredibly slow
manner, staring absentmindedly at the tablecloth. Finally she
got up and said she was going to have a nap. Better if I didn't
go out; the light was glaring and the hot sun was bad for the
digestion, we'd see each other at teatime. Flora finished washing the dishes and then went out into the little porch off the
kitchen, where she dozed off during the heat of the early
afternoon. The clock struck two and the afternoon loomed up
like a huge puddle of light and silence, interrupted by the
chirring of grasshoppers. I thought again of writing to ask my

father to take me away. But would he reply? What if the letter came back to me, bearing the inscription "unknown"? What would Clelia say, what sort of a story would she make up? Doubtless she'd say that my father wasn't like hers, like the Constantine Dragases, who sent her a facsimile of his feet in order to meet her memories halfway; my father was indifferent to any message, completely out of reach. What an idea! Why shouldn't my father reply? He'd reply, of course he would. I'll come right away, little boy; I realize that house is no place for your holidays. I'll take the earliest train next Saturday or, better still, I'll buy a car, a red Aprilia like the one you saw in front of the Andrea Doria Bathhouse. I know you took a shine to that car and you expect me to arrive sooner or later with one like it. Yes, I'll go and get a handsome car and call for you, if not this coming Saturday then the next Saturday or the one after, have no fear; sooner or later you'll see me turn up . . .

Cece slipped out of the kitchen door and looked around, seeming undecided about what to do, and I pretended to be asleep and didn't budge. He chased a fly and wheeled around several times, then came to a halt, bewildered, and made for the stairs. What if he were to start up them? The very idea made me break into a cold sweat. I imagined the commotion, Clelia's outcry and the crisis that might well follow. I had to stop him. But I mustn't touch him, Clelia had made that clear: to touch him meant breaking the spell, and besides it was very dangerous. Luckily Cece turned back, wrinkled up his nose at the carpeting of the stairway, tested his claws on it and began to whirl madly around chasing his tail. Then, with three joyful leaps, he made for the front door and went out into the garden. I followed him, not so much out of curiosity as just for something to do. The afternoon promised to be empty and lifeless, and there was no use writing to my father; he knew what I wanted and sooner or later he'd arrive with the red car. Only why had there had to be a war? Better not think about it and simply enjoy the day, including the sight of that stupid cat, so stupid that he was actually funny; he ran, leaping, after a butterfly, so heedlessly that he wound up in a rose bush. He didn't like that, and he arched his back, furiously, as if a dog were attacking him. I gave a low bark, trying not to disturb the people in the house, but it was quite enough to terrify him to the point where his fur stood on end. Stupid little kitten trying to imitate a grown cat! Unexpectedly he veered to one side in the direction of the wall. I realized that he was running away and tried to coax him back. Cece, Cece, come here, kitty . . . but it was too late. He slipped through the fancy ironwork of the gate and crossed the road. I saw the accident happen, with the impressive deliberateness of a slow-motion film. The man on the scooter was approaching, at a low speed, on the right-hand side of the road. Cece had stopped at the edge, uncertain whether or not to cross. The man saw his indecision and moved over to the white line in the middle of the road. At this point Cece lunged forward, but stopped halfway across. The man wavered, then returned to the right. Cece remained motionless, then turned back just when the scooter was only a few yards away. The man leaned dangerously to one side in order not to hit him, but did hit, or rather, graze him. Cece jumped backwards and slipped through the gate, miaowing and dragging an injured paw behind him. The scooter described a zigzag path—fortunately nothing was coming in the opposite direction—until the handlebars escaped from the rider's hands and it turned clear around; the mudguard scraped the cement, raising a stream of sparks, and the man rolled two or three times over on the ground as far as the lamppost. He got up quickly, and I saw that he was not badly hurt, even if he was in a scary condition, his trousers torn, one knee swollen and his hands bloody. Flora, awakened by the sound the scooter made when it ran against the wall, was the first to arrive on the scene. She went straight to the man and took him into the house. Aunt Esther soon followed. Not Clelia, no, she must be behind the curtains of her bedroom window, in a state of terror, and didn't come down; I could imagine what she'd have to say to me.

That danger more than ever hung over us, that everything was worse than before, that the real guilty party must be struck . . . it had to be done and Saturday was only forty-eight hours off. The suitcase dragged out again from under the bed, her thin hands with the bitten nails working over the white suit of that curious doll with the bow tie and the smile. . . . How do you like him, tell me. Doesn't he remind you of somebody? Now we take this string, we have to make knots, a little knot here, a little knot there, and you must repeat this word after me, no, not like that, silly, but as if you meant it, otherwise it won't work. And finally that big pin, brandished like a dagger in search of the right place to strike—the eyes, the heart, the throat . . . we had to decide. And what did I advise? I advised nothing, I didn't want to advise. It was no longer a game, the way it was in other years, a game to pass the summer away.

On Saturday evening Uncle Tullio took us to the Bathhouse. *Son of Tarzan* was no longer playing; there was only a film we couldn't see because minors weren't allowed, but we had a fine walk, all the finer because Clelia had consented to come along. Aunt Esther was radiant, you could read it on her face. We stayed late so as to hear the band. Aunt Esther ordered a fancy ice cream and Clelia and I sat among the potted palms, listening to *Mamma solo per te la mia canzone vola* and picking up the caps from bottles of Recoaro, which bore the same design as that on the T-shirts worn at championship soccer matches. Aunt Esther and Uncle Tullio danced on the platform bordered with potted palms and then we went home by the shore road. It was a beautiful evening and the tree-lined road was quiet and cool. Aunt Esther and Uncle Tullio walked briskly, arm in arm, and Clelia hummed as if she were happy. I felt as if we were back in the summers that had gone before, when everything was yet to happen. I

wanted to hug my aunt and uncle or write to my father not to
come for me, to pay no heed to my wish to see him arrive in a
red car, because I was content with things the way they were.
But Clelia tugged at my sleeve and said: It'll happen tomorrow, you'll see.

But on the morrow nothing happened. The morning was
superb and we went to the nine o'clock Mass so as to avoid the
noonday heat. Aunt Esther had a headache—because of the
follies of the night before, she said contritely—but her eyes
were shining with joy. Flora had made a fish chowder and the
house was filled with an appetizing smell. Cece was conva-
lescing in princely style in his basket and Flora was thrilled
because there was a film at the Don Bosco with her favourite
actress, Yvonne Sanson. Sunday dinner was a better occasion
than any in a long time, filled with laughing and chatter.
Then Aunt Esther went to take her nap, saying we'd meet
again at teatime. Uncle Tullio had something to do in the
garage; if I wanted to go with him he'd show me how to take
the distributor apart. I shot a glance at Clelia, but I couldn't
make out if there was any danger involved. I liked the idea of
fooling around with the distributor, but I didn't want to cause
Clelia any worry and so I said yes, I'd be glad to serve as
assistant mechanic, but not for too long, because Clelia and I
were reading a very exciting book, which we wanted to finish.
As I said these words I broke out into perspiration. But Uncle
Tullio didn't notice, he was pleased with the way the day was
going. In the garage he put on a pair of rubber gloves so as not
to dirty his hands and opened up the hood. Here's the engine
block, here's the dynamo, here's the fan, there are the spark
plugs . . . give me the toolbox, it's on the workbench over
there to the right. To take apart the distributor all you do is
press on the two springs, then use the screwdriver to loosen
these two screws, that's it, very good, just be careful not to pull
too hard so you won't snap the wires. It was a fine car, not
brand-new like my father's Aprilia, but nothing to turn up

your nose at; it could get up to a hundred and ten kilometers an hour. I worked until four o'clock, when I went into the house, leaving Uncle Tullio with his head still buried in the engine. Flora was probably sleeping in the deck chair on the back porch; she'd be going to see the film that evening and she wouldn't want to doze off in the middle. Cece was lying under the small sofa in the entrance hall, sticking his head out every once in a while. I tiptoed upstairs and knocked softly at Clelia's door. Everything's going right, she said, with an incomprehensible gesture, he suspects nothing, it seems to me, what do you think? I said it seemed to me, too, that he suspected nothing, but wouldn't it be wise to think twice about it? Uncle Tullio was such a good fellow, and our game was turning into something . . . something evil; she'd have to forgive the word, but that was what I honestly thought. Clelia looked at me in silence; the house was silent and even the usual noises from the shore were lacking. I wished that someone, anyone, would give signs of life—Aunt Esther, Flora, Cece—but there wasn't a sound and I was afraid even to breathe. Because now there was no way of turning back, everything was ready, and only an hour was left before the appointed time; the hands of the clock in the entrance hall were ticking away, inexorably. Then I said: I'll go down. But an indeterminate time had gone by when I said it; I was sitting on the rug near the half-open window and I had dreamed—or was dreaming—my father was driving along the shore in a red car and smiling at me. He was smiling at the wind, but the smile was meant for me and I was sitting there, waiting, and at the same time I saw him and waved my hand to tell him to stop. Then Clelia touched my shoulder and said let's go, and I followed her down the stairs as if I were somewhere else. In the dining room Flora had set the table for tea, so quietly that no one could hear; there were the teapot, the pitcher of lemonade, the toast and biscuits. Clelia sat down and I followed her example; Flora arrived promptly and said that the grown-ups would be there in a minute and we could begin. Uncle Tullio came in from the garden and Flora went upstairs to call Aunt Esther. She knocked at the door on the balcony and said: Signora, tea is ready. I was just starting to butter a piece of toast when Flora cried out. She was at the doorway of Aunt Esther's room, holding one hand over her mouth as if to prevent herself from crying out again, but another shrill, choked moan of horror and despair broke out of her throat. Clelia got up, overturning a cup of tea, and started to run towards the stairs, but Uncle Tullio prevented her. He, too, had got up and was looking with stupor at Flora, all the time holding Clelia close to him as if to protect her. I saw that she had taken off her glasses and her eye was rolling dizzily. She looked at me in a terrible manner, with an expression of terror and nausea and also of bewilderment on her face, as if she were silently begging for my help. But how could I help her, what could I do? Write to my father? I would have done that, with all my heart, but my father wasn't like Constantine Dragases. From where he was he couldn't send me even a facsimile of his feet to meet my memories halfway.

ROOMS

Amelia looked at the light veil of mist, descending in the distance, over the roof of the house, and thought: it's late, we've got to hurry. The path was steep and winding, paved with wide strips of granite; in the evening dampness it was like a petrified stream. There were clumps of rosemary and sage on either side; the air was cool and intensely fragrant and the hillside was carpeted with yellow splotches. October's here again, thought Amelia; perhaps tomorrow we'll have our first day of rain. Amelia always talked to herself in the first person plural; it was a habit she'd had for years, and if she had stopped to reflect, she wouldn't have been able to say when it had begun. She had lingered longer than she should at the organ and this gave her a twinge of worry. But it was irresistible, so much did she enjoy practising Pergolesi in the deserted church. Vespers were over, the little old women had drifted away, and the priest always let her be the one to finally shut the small side door, which closed with a click behind her. In the adjacent rectory the windows were already lit up; over the countryside the light had taken on the deepening blue colour of approaching night. We played much too well, Amelia said to herself, and quickened her steps.

From the churchyard she could see nothing of her house but the roof and the top-floor windows. The vine that climbed its twisting way up to the window sills was already half bare in preparation for the autumn, and there was a dim light in Guido's window from the shaded lamp on the bedside table. Beside the brass lamp, on the yellowed lace cloth, there were a Dante with a gilt binding like that of a Book of Hours, a crystal bottle marked off to indicate the dose of medicine for minor crises, an ivory box containing a mother-of-pearl rosary and a horn of red coral. As Amelia walked she reviewed these objects in her mind with the total recall born of long acquaintance with the detailed topography of a given room. A walnut cabinet occupied the far wall. In it her mother had kept the household linens and Amelia still used it for the heavy, yellowed sheets which had enveloped the sleep of preceding generations. Once upon a time the cabinet had had a key that stood out, for its large size, among the bunch hung from a nail in the wardrobe, with tags specifying, in brown ink, *pantry, cupboard, clothes closet, storage room.* To the right of the cabinet there was a small, marble-topped table where, when he was well enough to get up, Guido had sat to write, looking out of the window at the treetops and the slope of the hill. In a folding chessboard, in the right-hand drawer, Guido kept a diary, which, for years, Amelia had read every morning, comparing her impressions of the day before with those of her brother. She thought how bogus all writing really was—the implacable tyranny of circumscribing words, of verbs and adjectives that imprison things, hardening them into a glassy fixity, like a dragonfly caught for centuries in a rock, which keeps the appearance of a dragonfly but is one no longer. Such is writing, with its capacity to pin down the present and the recent past and distance them, by centuries, from us. But things are fuzzy-edged, thought Amelia; they are alive because they are fuzzy-edged, without borders, and do not let themselves be imprisoned by words.

The books of a lifetime were lined up on the table. Some

were bound in old leather, others in cardboard processed to
look like blue marble with ash-coloured veins running
through it: the New Testament, an eighteenth-century *Aeneid*
printed in Paris by the Frères Michaud, Tasso's *Aminta*,
Petrarch, Shelley, the lyrical poems of Goethe, Manzoni's *Adel-
chi*, Alfieri's *Vita*. In the upper right-hand corner of the blank
page before the frontispiece there was the owner's bookplate:
the sepia picture of a lighthouse throwing its beam over a
night-time sea and beneath it, in italics, *guido* with a small *g*.

In the left-hand drawer, tied together with ribbons of various
colours, were all the letters that Guido had received in the
course of his life. Amelia had, for years, kept them organized,
cataloguing them in order of importance: Academy, University,
Italian and foreign writers, magazines, appeals for aid. Some
began: *Dear Master and Friend*, others simply: *Your Excellency*,
in a pompous and fluttery hand. During the recent months of
his illness, there were only a few letters from tried-and-true
friends and a formal one from the Academy, expressing concern
for his health and wishing him a speedy recovery. To this
Amelia had replied with a polite short note: "My brother is not
able to answer you personally for the moment. I appreciate your
generous thought."

On the chest of drawers, with a mirror, next to the window,
there were photographs, mostly of Guido and herself, with one
of their mother as a child. Amelia had chosen to keep those of
their father and mother together on the chest in her own room.
As she walked, Amelia looked at the photographs and thought
about how time goes by. Time goes by. In the first photograph
Guido was twelve years old, wearing a grown-man's jacket and
short velveteen trousers, buttoned at the knee. His feet were
enclosed in high-buckled boots, the right one propped up on a
tree stump intended by the photographer to produce a rustic
air. On the backdrop there was an incongruous balcony giving
onto something like the bay of Naples, without the pine trees or
Vesuvius. In the lower right-hand corner was the handwritten
signature: Savinelli, Photo Studio.

Amelia looked at the photograph beside it, where already ten years had gone by. It was in a silver frame with a winding mark around the edges from the humidity, like the line left by a wave on the shore. Guido was at Amelia's left, offering her his right arm, on which she leaned lightly, like a bride. He was wearing a dark suit and a wide tie and his left hand was holding his hat, by the rim, against his thigh. She was wearing a white, slightly fluffy dress with a ribbon around the waist. A straw hat shaded her forehead all the way down to the barely visible eyes, but the rest of her face was flooded with light and an ingenuous, perhaps happy smile revealed a row of white teeth. It was summer and behind them the pergola, overgrown with grape-vines, outlined puddles of shade in the courtyard. On the wrought-iron table there was a pitcher, which someone had filled with flowers. Brother and sister seemed like a bride and groom immediately after the ceremony. Yes, on the day when Guido received his university degree, there was a party under the pergola; Amelia remembered it perfectly. Father and mother weren't yet dead; father had overdone it with the food and drink and now he was sitting in the shade of the porch, his face shiny and his waistcoat unbuttoned so that his big paunch could be seen rising and falling under his shirt as he drew breath. Father, thought Amelia, overcome by nostalgia. She had no such nostalgia for her mother; she thought of her with little or no sorrow, only with a faint regret faded by memory. She was a pale, slight, silent woman, who tiptoed through the house and through life. She had died early, before Amelia knew what real sorrow was, leaving almost imperceptible traces: the memory of her rustling skirt and pale hands, of the way she brushed her long hair, which she camouflaged in a braid rolled up at the nape of her neck. Father, on the other hand, had a loud voice, his footsteps rang out through the house and he filled it with his presence. He gave her big hugs which made for a feeling of safety and for a strange warmth, which caused her to blush.

Amelia was aware of hating this photograph. She learned to hate it years later, when hatred no longer made sense. She knew and preferred not to know the real reason. In that faraway moment captured by the lens she preferred to think that what annoyed her were insignificant details: her own infantile, almost stupid smile, the slope of Guido's right shoulder, indicative, perhaps, of embarrassment, yes, insignificant things. And then there were two other photographs beside it, which she didn't hate; they were part of her real life, after the choices had been made. Yes, the choices.

What choices? Amelia asked as she walked along, pushing away the shoot of a blackberry bush which had fallen across the path. For some time now she had carried a cane; not that she was so old, she walked perfectly well without support, but she liked to go out on Sunday afternoons with the cane that had belonged to her father, a slender, elegant bamboo cane, with a silver knob in the shape of a small dog's head. What choices?

In the third photograph Guido had a solemn, ceremonious expression. He was wearing an academic gown and holding a rolled-up parchment in one hand while with the other he leaned on the edge of a dry fountain in the University cloisters. The last photograph had been taken at an official dinner where Guido, as guest of honour, was seated at the head of the table. It had been snapped when the dinner was nearly over and wine had dissolved the artificial solemnity of the participants' faces, leaving them relaxed and defenceless. There were writers and artists; the scrawny little man at the end of the table was a famous musician whom she had always found as insipid as his compositions. She was at her brother's right hand; her eyes reflected satisfaction and contentment, but her lips had narrowed in comparison with those in her eighteen-year-old image. They had lost their openness and generosity, they were tight, cautious, watchful of words, thoughts, and life.

Time is very strange.

"Signor Guido has had an attack," Cesarina told her in a low voice. "The pain must have been unbearable, because he bit his hands so that he wouldn't cry out, then he moaned like an animal. Now he's dozed off; he couldn't stand it any longer."

Cesarina was a young, married woman with a peaches-and-cream complexion and enormous breasts, a creature of milk and blood. She had brought her last-born baby with her and laid him to sleep in a straw basket on a shelf on the kitchen cabinet. He was a quiet child, who woke up only when he was hungry, and she nursed him, perching on a high stool. She had taken her mother's place in the household. Her mother's name was Fanny, and she had spent her whole life in the family's service. Fanny was the same age as Amelia and, as children, they had played together. If Amelia had married she might now have a daughter of Cesarina's age—this thought occasionally crossed her mind—and a couple of grandchildren.

Now she told Cesarina thanks; she would take over. This had become a regular thing. The girl should go home; it was late and the road to the village was dark and riddled with holes. She answered the girl's goodnight and picked up the pitcher of water. "The soup's ready," Cesarina added. "I made a light beef broth." As Amelia went up the stairs she heard the sound of the garden gate opening and closing. After that there was only the faint sound of her own footsteps. A ray of dim light filtered through the crack of the door to Guido's room; as she went by she heard his laboured, lugubrious breathing. Gingerly she opened the adjacent door of her own room and gingerly shut it, with the old wood barely creaking behind her. She took off her coat in the darkness and hung it on the three-legged coat-stand beside the door. On the chest of drawers a perpetual light burned before the photograph of her father and mother, two ancient faces against a faded background, smiling at nothingness. In the semi-darkness she reached for her dressing gown and opened the window. The air was sharp and the moon, rising over the hill, cast a halo, broken only by the trees. Amelia stretched out on the bed, still looking out into the night. This was her parents' bed; here, many years ago, two people had conceived her. The bed stood against the wall which divided it from Guido's bed. Just so, they had been divided by a wall for so long a time. Amelia thought of this and then, again, of time. She could almost hear it glide by, now that the countryside lay sleeping in silence; it hummed with the sound of a subterranean river. She thought of how many nights she had slept in this bed, thinking of the person asleep on the other side of the wall. And she thought of hate. Hate, too, is a fuzzy-edged, elusive thing, it refuses to be imprisoned by words, it has multiple shapes, shadings, fringes, paces, fluxes and refluxes and imperceptible shifts between light and darkness. Hate can make you wish somebody would die. For a long time, in secret, she had nursed such a wish. She couldn't say when it had started, for hate has a strange way of taking concrete shape. Before it becomes definite and definable it has already been born within us, it silently pre-existed, hidden in some recess of the mind. And then, perhaps it wasn't hate after all. Amelia thought of the expression: recesses of the mind. How very apt it was, for the mind has many recesses.

A sharp wail, almost a whistle, came through the wall. This was how Guido woke up when the pain was upon him. Then the wail turned into something heartrending, a whine, punctuated by massive and fearful outcries in the night. Amelia got up and lit the lamp. On the linen cloth covering the toilet table the metal box containing the sterilized syringe, the alcohol and the vials was ready. Now Guido was awake and scratching the wall with a finger; the nail had dug out a furrow in the plaster above his bed. With a small metal saw Amelia opened a vial. She took the syringe from the box and squirted out the water left in the needle. Then she sucked up the contents of the vial, before pointing the syringe upward and pumping out the last air bubbles. Finally she dipped a wad of cotton into the bottle of alcohol and squeezed it out. "I'm coming, Guido," she called out. She thought of the meaning of pity and knew that her hands were administering it. There was an emptiness in her breast, like an icy tunnel. But the hands holding the syringe were steady, without a shiver, without a tremor.

ANY WHERE OUT
OF THE WORLD

The way things happen! And what determines their course. A trifle. Sometimes it can start with a trifle, with a fragmentary phrase lost in this great world full of phrases and things and faces, in a big city like this one, with squares and subway lines and people hurrying away from their jobs, with trams, cars, parks, and then the placid river. Towards sunset, boats glide down to the river's mouth, where the city widens into a sprawling, low-roofed, white suburb, with great empty spaces, like eye sockets, among the houses. Vegetation is scarce and there are shoddy little cafés where you can eat standing up, looking at the lights along the coast or seated at rusty red wrought-iron tables that make a scraping sound on the pavement, served by waiters with weary faces and soiled white jackets. Sometimes I wander around there in the evening. I take a slow tram which goes down the Avenida and then wanders through the narrow, crooked streets until it runs along the river. As if it were in a race between two asthmatics, it vied against the tugboats on the other side of the embankment, so close you could reach out and touch them. There are old wooden telephone booths with, occasionally, someone inside—an old woman who seems to have seen better days, a railway worker, a sailor, and I wonder: with whom are they talking? Then the tram circles the Navy Museum, around a square containing three century-old palm trees and stone benches. Poor children play poor children's games, the same as in my own childhood, skip-rope or hopscotch.

On this particular evening I got off the tram and started to walk, with my hands in my pockets and my heart pounding; I didn't know why, unless it was the effect of the simple music coming out of an old gramophone in a certain café, always a waltz in F major or a fado played on the accordion. Here I am, I thought, and nobody knows me; I'm a nameless face among a multitude of nameless faces, nameless here or anywhere else, and this thought caused me torment and a feeling of splendid and superfluous freedom, like that of rejected love. And then I thought nobody knows, nobody suspects anything, nobody can blame me; here I am, scot-free, I can even imagine that nothing happened if I want to. I looked at my reflection in a window. Do I look guilty? I adjusted the knot of my tie and pushed back my hair. My appearance was good, a little weary, perhaps, or slightly sad. Anyone would take me for a man who's lived his life—nothing special, the usual thing, with some good points and some bad, all of which have left their mark on his face as on any other. Of the rest there's nothing to be seen. This too gave me a feeling of splendid and superfluous freedom, just as when you've wanted for ages to do something and finally you've done it. And what was I to do now? Nothing, just nothing. Sit down at a table in that café, stretch out your legs ("Bring me an orange juice and some almonds, thank you"), open the newspaper, which you bought quite lackadaisically since you've little interest in the news. Sporting Lisbon tied with Real Madrid in the championship cup, the price of shellfish is going up, the government crisis seems to have been staved off, the mayor has approved the plan to create a pedestrian area in the historical centre of the city, with flower-boxes in the middle of this or that street so that here

there will be an oasis for walking and shopping; in some town
up north a bus ran off the street and into a corner shop
because the driver suddenly had a heart attack and died, not
from running into the shop but from a thrombosis; there were
no other victims, only damage to the shop which was completely wiped out—it was a shop that carried wedding and
first-communion gifts. Then you look at the job offers, but
with little interest since the Language School pays well, is
close to where you live and takes up only five hours a day; the
rest of the time is yours. You can stroll, read and write (something you've always enjoyed) or else go to see your favourite
films, from the 1950s, you might even give private lessons, like
some of your colleagues, if you could endure teaching listless
children from good families, for a good fee. Anyhow, let's
have a look; you never can tell. Food products firm, centrally
located, seeks salesman good knowledge French, English,
P.O. Box 199. Import-export business with Latin America,
knowledge English, Spanish, accounting experience preferred. Swiss pharmaceutical house opening city office, German
language essential, diploma in chemistry. Shipping company, Bangkok–Hong Kong–Macao line, custody and delivery
of merchandise, must be willing to travel. And then the mov-
ies. Why not? Tomorrow's your free day and you can stay out
late, even for the midnight show. First a snack down the river
at the Port of Santa Maria, shrimp in a sweet-sour sauce and
Cantonese rice. There's a John Ford festival—wonderful—
where you can catch *The Horse Soldiers* (a bit of a bore), *Rio
Grande*, and *A Yellow Ribbon*. The alternative is a French
retrospective, slow-moving intellectual films and the com-
plexities of Marguerite Duras, no thanks. Somewhere they're
showing *Casablanca*, oh yes, at the Alpha Cinema, never
heard of it, must be at the ends of the earth, on a street
nobody's ever heard of. What did Ingrid Bergman do when
she came to Lisbon and saw "The End" flashed on the screen?
The story should have a sequel, said the reviewer. I know him,

a fellow my age with a black moustache and keen eyes, who also writes short stories. But perhaps you're tired. It must be the humidity. Sometimes a heavy fog rolls in from the Atlantic, penetrates and stops up the pores of your skin and makes your legs feel like two sticks. At the Capitol there's a reissue of the Duke Jordan record, *Sultry Eva* and *Kiss of Spain*; you remember it perfectly, from Paris, 1964. It was icy cold and you lived on sandwiches; *she* was still to come, in the mists of the future. Now the Personals; they're the most interesting because humanity lays itself bare, pitifully hiding behind euphemism. It's pitiful, yes, the veil of words. Trustworthy widow seeks a lasting friendship. Three special ads with indecipherable abbreviations. A retired man who's perishing from loneliness. The usual matchmaking agency: why haven't you come to us to find a kindred spirit? And then, all of a sudden your heart begins to pound furiously, tap, tap, tap; you can hear it in your throat and the people at the other tables must hear it as well. The world loses shape, everything is opaque, lights and sounds fade away, as if an immense, unnatural silence had paralyzed the universe. You look again at the little phrase, you re-read it, there's a strange taste in your mouth; it's not possible you think, it's a horrible coincidence and then you take back the word "horrible" and think: it's only a coincidence, a matter of chance, one little chance among millions, just a happening. But why is it happening to you, that's what you ask yourself, and why in this place, at this table, in this newspaper? It's not possible; you think, it's a dislocated phrase, a slug that was mislaid at the printer's, under hundreds of others, and which a careless linotypist pulled out by mistake and put into the want ads. You formulate this hypothesis and others which are even more absurd: they gave me an old paper, by mistake I bought one four years old. The newspaper vendor had it under the counter, it had been there four years and when he saw that I was a foreigner he palmed it off on me; it's all a cheap trick,

not worth losing your head about. In an embarrassed and
clumsy manner you turn back to the first page to find the date,
blaming the sea breeze for ruffling the pages and preventing
you from folding them back neatly. Of course you're not
nervous, you're perfectly cool and collected; keep cool now.
It's today's paper, the paper of this day and of this year in the
Gregorian calendar. Yes, today's. *Any where out of the world.*
You re-read the phrase a dozen times over; this isn't a regular
advertisement, it's a paid, clandestine message in the evening
paper, with no mention of a post-office box, a name, address,
business, school. Only this: *Any where out of the world.* And
you need to know nothing more, because the phrase drags
after it, the way a flooded river carries flotsam in its wake, bits
and pieces of words which your memory, with a frightening,
icy calm, is putting into order. *This life is a hospital where
every patient wants to change beds. One would prefer to suffer
near the stove, another thinks he can be cured beside the
window.* "Your orange juice, sir. Sorry, there are no more
almonds. Would you care for some other kind of nut?" You
make a gesture that might mean either yes or no, wanting not
to be interrupted, because now you are looking at the coast,
where the lights are once more visible to your eyes, and words
and memories too, are lit up in your mind, to the point that
you can almost see them shine; they are little lights in the
night, obviously far away, and yet you could pick them up
and hold them in the palm of your hand. *It always seems to
me that I should be better off where I am not, and this
question of packing up and moving is one which I ceaselessly
debate with my soul.* You've picked up your glass and are
taking little sips of juice. You seem a quiet, somewhat dreamy
customer, looking, like the customers at other tables, at the
river and the night. You've folded the newspaper and laid it
carefully on the table in the exaggeratedly meticulous manner
of certain old men who have borrowed a paper from the
barber and have to give it back. You look at it with distracted

indifference; it's only a paper, after all, today's paper, carrying already stale news, because the day is over and someone, somewhere, is already making up another paper with news that will shortly dispossess the news, coagulated into words, of today. But today's sheet carries an item four years old and yet very new, disquietingly new. If you were to give in, it would greatly upset you; but you're not going to give in, you can't, you must stay cool. Only then do you notice the date—the twenty-second of September. A coincidence, you say to yourself again. But a coincidence with what? An impossible second coincidence, not only of words but also of dates, the same date and the same phrase. And nothing can stop it; it's as if it had a voice of its own in your memory, like a clinging childish singsong which you thought you'd shaken off because it had been engulfed in the past, but it hadn't really disappeared; it lay in a deep recess within you, until now its rhythm is re-awakened and its phrasing begins to drip, tic, tic, tic—it pushes against a rocky wall, it buzzes and gropes for an outlet, then bursts forth like a spring, bathing you in tepid water, which somehow makes you shiver, and finally pulls you into its eddies with a power that it's useless to resist, violently and irresistibly whirling through subterranean tunnels as it leads you on. *Tell me, dear heart, dear chilled heart, what would you say to going to live in Lisbon? It's surely warm there and you'd revive like a lizard under the sun. The city's at the water's edge and they say it's built of marble. You see it is a country after my own heart; a landscape made up of light and stone, and water to reflect them!* And so you walk slowly through this marble city, between eighteenth-century buildings and arcades that witnessed the days of colonial trade, sailing ships, the bustle and the foggy dawns of anchors being weighed. Your solitary footsteps raise an echo; there's an old beggar leaning against a pillar, beyond the arches there's the square right on the river, licked by its muddy waters; the brightly lighted boats providing a ferry service to the opposite shore are taking off from the pier; soon the haste of the last passengers will be swallowed up by the dark, leaving only the silent night, peopled by a few distracted night-walkers—unquiet souls carrying their sleepless bodies around and talking to themselves. You talk to yourself, too, first in silence, then out loud, articulating your words very distinctly as if you were dictating them, as if the river could take them down and preserve them in some watery archive, amid the sand, pebbles, and rubbish of the sea floor. Until finally you say: *guilt.* A word you've never pronounced before, perhaps because you didn't have the nerve, and yet a simple, unequivocal word, which echoes clearly in the darkness and seems to enter, completely, into the halo of your breath, where it is condensed for a moment in the damp air before fading away. You enter the empty square; the monument is impressive and the tall rider spurs his horse into the night. *Guilt.* You sit on the base of the monument and light a cigarette; the folded newspaper is in your pocket and the mere feel of it gives you a sense of subtle discomfort, like the prick of a pin or an insect on the nape of your neck. It's not possible, nobody knows I'm here, I'm lost among the world's million faces; it can't be a message for me, it's only a phrase that many people know, it's another reader of Baudelaire who's secretly conveying a secret to somebody else. And for a moment you follow up the strange idea of a repetition, a doubling-up, as if it were plausible that the wheel of fate should possess stereotypes and print them out haphazardly, in the lives of other people with different eyes and hands and ways of being, in different streets and rooms. Another man, then, talking to another woman in another room, *a room that is like a dream.* And your fantasy creates the lighted window of a room that is itself a fantasy. You can approach the misted window and peek through the old lace curtains. It's a room with antique furniture, and wallpaper with a faded tulip design. A man and a woman are on the bed; it's evident from the position of the bodies and the rumpled sheets that they've been making love. He strokes her head and says: "Let me keep on breathing the scent of your hair." At that moment a clock strikes. "It's late," she says; "I must go." But you answer: "The Chinese tell time by a cat's eye. It's not time yet, Isabelle, everything has yet to happen: I've still to involve you in the real betrayal, but it won't be my fault, believe me, it's the fault of *things* that will it so—who knows what determines their course?—and you have still to let yourself be involved in the betrayal; but it won't be your fault either, and then, in my own way, I'll have to bring about your death, but this, too, won't be my fault. It will be your remorse, and meanwhile he'll know nothing of my betrayal, only one day a notice in the newspaper, a short, secret phrase, which only we two know—*Any where in the world*—will be the signal, and then everything will happen." Instead, everything had already happened, only the man in that room didn't know it and said: "You're right, it's late. Go along, and I'll go afterwards."

Now you leave the café and walk across the square. A prostitute in a car signals to you with the headlights but you shake your head, still thinking: it's not possible, it's just a coincidence, a trick of fate. But something tells you it's no such thing. A chill has penetrated your bones and its iciness is a sort of certainty; the cathedral clock rings out the same hour as a clock rang four years before, you think again that it's a repetition of the same story; perhaps I could eat something— I'm just cold and hungry. A tram goes by, but you don't want to get on. You prefer to go on foot up the steep street leading from the river to the castle; there are laughing foreign tourists and sightseeing buses and an Indian restaurant where you often go for a chicken *balchao*—the owner is a fellow from Goa who talks his head off, perhaps he drinks too much, but he makes a sauce that goes well with the rice and sometimes he serves a spiced wine. Two American couples are happily eating near the window; the table lamps have checked red-

and-white shades which make for a cosy, intimate atmosphere; the floor is somewhat dirty, with paper napkins that
have fallen from the tables and not been picked up. Senhor
Colva is less talkative than usual, he looks tired, perhaps
because the place has been too crowded. "The *balchao* may be
a bit spicy," he says. "I'll bring you some cold beer." He is
unfailingly attentive without a touch of servility. Then, with
the air of suddenly remembering something, he taps his forehead, as if to admit his forgetfulness and to beg pardon for it
at the same time. He walks, with short steps, over to the bar
and comes back smiling. "Your paper," he says. You stare at
the paper in his outstretched hand but do not reach out to take
it. You feel yourself turning pale and sweating cold sweat; you
touch your jacket. Your paper, neatly folded, is in the slightly
bulging pocket where you had put it. You look at the paper
that Senhor Colva is holding but do not reach out to take it.
What he reads on your face is only surprise, not the terror that
you feel like a stream of ants climbing from your ankles to
your groin. "They must have brought it for you," he says;
"you're the only one to read this particular paper." "Ah, yes,'
you manage to answer with frightening calm, "but who
brought it?" "I don't know, sir; my son found it this morning
under the door. There was a wrapping around it, of course,
but the rascal tore it off in order to read about the soccer
match. You know, don't you, that Sporting Lisbon tied with
Real Madrid?" You agree that this is an achievement, too bad
the game wasn't on TV. They say that Sporting deserved to
win if it hadn't been for the incident with the cross bar and, of
course, the referee; in such cases the referee is all-important,
although Real have a very fine pitch and fans who are perfect
gentlemen . . . but was he sure that your name was on the
wrapping of this paper? He looked around, puzzled. You'll
have to forgive the boy, today young people don't know how
to behave; in his time it was different, they got the whip. He
put on a serious expression and retreated with his quick short

steps to the back of the room. Just before the kitchen there was
a stairway leading to his living quarters. You know perfectly
well that your name wasn't on the wrapping although you
can't be certain for the simple reason that something of this
kind is without certainty or explanation, that's the truth; and
then you begin to ponder what it *really* means to demand an
explanation of something like that which is happening. Or
an explanation of all that did happen, yes, all, getting to the
bottom of it—she, he, you, and the pinwheel of subterfuges,
postponements, and confusions which go to make up the
whole story. Then you begin to allot the moral responsibili-
ties, and that's the worst thing of all because it leads nowhere;
as you well know, life can't be measured in moral terms, it
simply happens. But he didn't deserve it. That's certain. And
she knew that he didn't deserve it. Equally certain. And you
knew that she knew that he didn't deserve it, and you didn't
care. Yes, but why shouldn't you have deserved to stay with
her? You met her only later, much later, didn't you, that's
true, too—it was after all the chips were down. But what
chips? Life has no such deadlines, no croupier who raises his
hand to indicate that the chips are down to stay; everything
moves on and nothing stands still. Why should we remain
apart after we'd found each other, as the real game seemed to
have decreed: the same tastes—white houses with scrawny
palm trees or scarce vegetation, agaves, tamarinds, a rock; the
same passions—Chopin or minimalist music, old rumbas,
Tiengo el corazon maluco; the same nostalgia—the *spleen de
Paris*. Let's get away from this place and this spleen and look
for a city of white marble at the water's edge; let's look together for such a city or another like it, it doesn't matter
where, anywhere out of the world. "I can't." "Yes, you can, if
you want to." "Please don't force me." "I'll send you a message. I'm leaving, I've already left, I can't stand it any longer,
join me if you choose, buy this paper, it will be the signal and
tell you where to find me, leave everything, no one will

know." No one *can* know, you're thinking while Senhor
Colva makes an apologetic gesture from the back of the restaurant, which you wave away. You and she were the only
ones to know, and Baudelaire. You played a game with him,
too—certain things aren't to be fooled around with; you
musn't needle the mystery that brought them about. But no
one else knew, of this you're certain. He didn't know, that's
sure, and if he did know, it's ancient history. Because at
present everything's "ancient history": that's why your hands
shake as you pay the bill. It doesn't make any sense. Yet there
is some sense to it, you know this or rather feel it. And you
want to put it to the test. You go to the telephone near the
washroom, insert a coin, and dial that dead number. This too
is ancient history; the telephone company hasn't given it to
anyone else, so it hangs loose, a group of figures which
transmit an acoustic signal to nobody; you've known that all
too well for four years. You dial the number slowly, you hear
one, two, three rings, then the receiver clicks, but no voice
answers; you feel only a presence, not even a breath, because it
doesn't breathe. At the other end of the wire there's only a
presence which is there to listen to the presence of your silence. And so you hang up and go out onto the street. You've
no intention of going home, because you know that the telephone would ring, one, two, three times, you'd pick up the
receiver and hold it to your ear and there would be nothing
from the other end, only the distinct density of a presence
listening in silence to the silence of your presence. You go
back to the river; the boat traffic is suspended for the night
and the piers are deserted. You sit on the embankment wall,
the water is muddy and rippling; perhaps it's high tide and
the river can't work its way to the sea. You know that it's late,
but not merely by the clock; the hour around you is as vast and
solemn as space, a motionless unit of time which is not
marked on the dial and is as light as a sigh, as quick as a
glance.

BITTERNESS AND CLOUDS

"People do you good turns and you repay them with bitterness. Why?" He was reading the final tercet of the poem by Drummond de Andrade which he was in the process of analyzing, when that sentence, spoken one afternoon many years before, came back to mind. His first good suit, jacket and trousers, in brown gaberdine with a narrow yellow stripe, perfectly horrendous as he realized later, when he had learned how to dress, but at the time he thought it was close to perfect, or at least important looking—too good for the office but indispensable for a graduation. He had looked at his reflection in the window. It was a men's clothing shop on the Viale Libia, handling moderately priced but well-cut garments, and the minute he had put this suit on he felt at ease in it; perhaps it made him look a bit arrogant, but that didn't hurt. It's no good showing yourself to other people as submissive, that's the end. Bitterness. Call it, rather, the wellspring of his being, a way to avoid being eaten alive in this world of wolves. But he didn't answer Cecilia's question, there was no answer to give. She wouldn't have understood and the wolves had already eaten her up, wolves in the sense of life—you had only to look at her. At thirty years of age she was an old woman. Hair parted in the middle, some white strands already, a depressing air of resignation and her eternal fa-

tigue. What fault was it of his if a few years before he had been
in love with her and now he wasn't? Perhaps it had been not
so much love as a common purpose, their marriage had been
based on a common purpose and certainly *he* hadn't reduced
her to her present condition. And this was the reason for his
embitterment, the condition into which she had fallen, an
uncared-for face and a tired body. Which was an unconscious
way of displaying the sacrifices she had made on his behalf; a
lament, a reproach, a mediocre remonstrance which, in reality, perversely masked her deep frustration. But how was he to
blame for the defeat of a woman doomed to defeat? He had
done his best to back her up. The immediate post-war years
had been hard for both of them. There they were, in the uglier
outlying area of the big city, with their parents dead and no
one to turn to, wanting to set up house together if for no other
reason than to have company. What were they to do? Jobs in
the post office seemed the solution, but although these pro-
vided food and a roof over their heads, the atmosphere was
squalid. A wood-burning stove and mud puddles in front of
the door in the winter, humidity and mosquitoes in the
summer, and all the year around the dull faces of their fellow
employees, the widow who wasn't really a widow, the assistant supervisor who talked of nothing but soccer but never
bought a ticket to a match. Finally he had said: "Cecilia, let's
move on to something better, let's sign up at the university
and aim at a career." But she was always tired. And why, after
all? Wasn't he tired, too? They had the same working hours.
And the amount of housework she did—making the bed and
washing a few dishes—couldn't be called tiring. If the place
had been spick-and-span he might have understood her being
tired. But the three disorderly rooms, with her bedroom
slippers always sticking out from under the bed, didn't seem
appropriate to a young married couple; they were the preview
of an old people's home; he had never summoned up the
courage to ask even his sister to drop in.

And then Gianna was born, but that wasn't his fault either; she had wanted a child. "This isn't the moment," he had told her. "Let's wait, and time it better. A child's a burden, one that will swallow up what little free time we have." But she cried at night; the longing for motherhood consumed her like a fire and it must have been the only warmth within her because the rest was desert. Finally the silly woman struck a bargain. She'd take total care of the child and he could enrol at the university, he could even leave his job and devote his whole time to his studies. Since she'd had a promotion, her salary would be enough for them to live on and, if he didn't object, she'd do some moonlighting at home over the weekend; a private postal service was offering just such employment. He said all right, if that was what she wanted. He wasn't the one to stifle her maternal instinct, but it was agreed that he didn't have to change diapers. He'd spend weekends at the university library, where a friendly guard would let him in on Sundays. If she wanted a child, he wanted a university degree; they both had their priorities. The agreement was clear and he respected it. She did, too, silently and with no audible complaint, only her usual resignation. Job, housework, take-home assignments from the office, care of the child. The little girl was just like her mother, things happen that way; nature is implacable. The same apathy, the same resigned look, the same defeat written on her face. As she grew, on the rare Sundays when he didn't go to the library, he tried to awaken her interest in something, to rouse her from her precocious torpor. "Do you want to take a walk with Papa, to go to the zoo?" And the voice of a humble, common-sense little woman answered: "I must keep Mama company, thank you, Papa. She asked me to lend her a hand with the housework." And so there they were, at it, bolstering up his "privilege" of being a middle-aged student, toiling over his books late at night in order to keep up with the young classmates who appeared on Monday morning rested and casual, with neatly creased trousers and pullovers in the latest style, quite the young gentlemen. Of course he felt it in his heart to hate those young gentlemen. And this surge of feeling, tinged with bitterness and resentment, rose, again, from the depths of his being. His hatred of them was mute and inexpressible and only increased by the fact that they shared the same political stance. In their case there were rich fathers, a long liberal tradition, membership in the postwar *Partito d'Azione*. Their inherited political background was a luxury and their own left-wing views even more of one. For him, instead, they marked an achievement, a painful journey slowed by family considerations, respect for a church-going mother and father with too many children to support to be able to indulge in politics. His way of being a left-winger was based on first-hand acquaintance with want, the refusal to accept it, and, finally, revenge. This had nothing to do with their abstract, geometrical ideology. He had said as much, one day, to the most stupid among them, who voiced disapproval of his choice, for director of his thesis, of an unpopular and down-trodden professor known to harbour nostalgia for the days of the dictatorship. He had looked his fellow-student in the face and said, "It's all very easy for you to be on the left, my boy. You've no idea of the difficulties of real life." And the other had only stared at him with amazement.

The Professor. He wasn't a genius, no doubt of that. But more brilliant teachers had scowled when he asked their advice about a subject for his thesis. The Professor had shown immediate understanding of his situation as a middle-aged student and a father. "I hope, at least, that you're not like those presumptuous young fellows who, instead of recalling our country's heroic past, look only to a radiant future." And he had answered, cautiously: "Every form of government has its good points, Professor. It's only that today the past of which you are speaking is in total disrepute." Their under-standing, at least at the start, was based on mutual respect, and was advantageous to him. Working out his thesis didn't take too long; the worst part was the typing. He stayed up until all hours pecking away at a typewriter which Cecilia brought home every evening from the office. The reproachful look on her tired face was underlined by the hardship of carrying an old Olivetti, as big as a tank, up four flights of stairs while Gianna memorized geometry theorems in the kitchen. The rest went smoothly enough. Top marks for the oral exam; the thesis was substantial and the Professor, when he wanted to, could count on the support of some of his colleagues. Publication, too, turned out to be fairly easy, at the hands of a printer who also ran up university lectures and did not make the usual charge on this occasion. The dedication *To my Master* seemed useful as well as necessary. Bitterness came afterwards, when it was a question of a post as an assistant in the department. The Professor's talk had become less guarded and neutral. Gone were the days of mutual respect; he demanded approval and complicity.

When he left home, he did it in the most proper and painless manner, leaving a letter behind him. It was the day he got his first salary payment as an assistant. A pittance, but enough for one person to live on. He had found a room in an old building behind the hospital, very small, with a window overlooking a courtyard filled with stretchers. It was not attractive, and he spent a week whitewashing the walls and installing a table bought from a junk dealer, a chair, and a coat rack. There was already a bed; he had only to add a mattress. An outsider might have called the room a miserable affair, but he saw it as an example of sobriety. He thought often of Machado, who lived in a room like this one, with a table, a chair, a bed, and an iron washstand, in the boarding house kept by Doña Isabel Cuevas. He had read *Campos de Castilla* and found in it a spiritual affinity. Especially in the *Retrato* which opens the collection, with a sort of catalogue of events, sometimes anecdotal in character but at the same time allusive, summing up a whole life: restrained but firm ethical and ideological statements and a joking reference to his mode of dress. It was a Sunday afternoon and he sat at his work table, re-reading the *Retrato* for the nth time. First he underlined three lines and then transcribed them. *Mi historia, algunos casos que recordar no quiero. /Ya conosceis mi torpe alino indumentario. /Hay en mis venas gotas de sangre jacobina.* "My story, some events that I do not want to recall. / Already you know about my shabby clothes. /There are drops of Jacobin blood in my veins." Those lines, he thought, belonged to him personally, they could have been his own. And then he copied two more. He was looking out of the window at the hospital courtyard. It was May, and the slender trees were green. At one point, a nurse, holding a little girl by the hand, stepped out from a small iron gate bearing the word "Radiology" in a yellow triangle above it. They were advancing very slowly because the child's legs were encased in two metal braces all the way up to the hips. The legs were scrawny, rigid and deformed, and she walked with obvious difficulty, as if imitating the pathetically grotesque waddle of a duck. She seemed no more than eight years old, with fair hair and a checked dress. The nurse sat her down on a stretcher, tapped her on one cheek, made a reassuring gesture indicating that she should be patient, and then went away. The girl sat there patiently, looking at the empty courtyard, while the nurse re-entered the hospital. At this moment a white cat came out of the opposite corner. Hard to say whether the cat or the child was the first to see the other. They exchanged stares and then the cat trotted towards her like a puppy and jumped nimbly onto the stretcher, where the little girl took him into her arms and kissed him. He lowered his eyes to the poem before him and re-read the line *Mi historia, algunos casos que recordar no quiero.* He saw that the printed words were quivering through his tears and, in his notebook, added three more lines to those he had already copied: *Pero mi*

*verso brota de manatial sereno /Y, mas que un hombre al uso
que sabe su doctrina /Soy, en el buen sentido de la palabra,
bueno* [But my verse flows from a source serene/ and, rather
than an everyday man who knows his doctrine,/ I am, in the
best sense of the word, good].

That summer he made a trip to Spain and Portugal. The
Professor, through the "Friends of Spain", got him a grant
from the Spanish Ministry of Foreign Affairs. There were no
strings attached; it was an invitation, a reward for his interest
in Spanish culture. Spaniards were proud of their culture and
flattered if scholars from foreign universities wanted to con-
sult their libraries. The only obligation which he incurred
was the delivery of the proofs of an article written by the
Professor for a review in Madrid to which he was a contribu-
tor. It was a no-account review, but that wasn't his affair.
Barcelona overwhelmed him. An immense, sunlit city with
tree-lined boulevards, splendid late nineteenth-century buildings and cordial and affable people—the city which had suf-
fered the worst damage during the civil war. After ten days he
felt that he belonged there. His heart, his very nature were
akin to those of the people who thronged, in the evening, to
the lower part of the city, the harbour, the cafés, the wine
shops, and the sordid taverns in the alleyways. It irked him to
have to stay in the luxury hotel where he was put up by the
Ministry of Foreign Affairs. While he took his dinner in the
brightly lighted dining room, in the company of well-dressed
travellers eating shellfish, he longed to be among the simple,
noisy folk in the taverns which he had glimpsed during his
afternoon walks, drinking in, with an almost physical pleasure, the liquid Catalan speech, so different from the dry
sonority of the Castilian. All of this reinforced his anti-Franco
feelings. His heart was unequivocally with the victims of the
war; he remembered, suddenly, all that they had endured and
was deeply moved by it. He decided, on the spot, to learn
Catalan, as a tribute to Catalonia. Meanwhile he thought of

another tribute, the book by Orwell, which he had read on the train and thrown into a rubbish bin at the frontier railway station, because it was the tribute of an English snob, of the same class as the travellers eating shellfish at his hotel, people who knew nothing of the soul of the common people of Spain. He felt more and more bitterness towards certain false progressives of his acquaintance and boundless affection for the crystal-clear figure of Dolores Ibarruri. She was the earthy embodiment of the Spanish people, she was generosity and self-sacrifice in person. La Pasionaria! He really should have gone to Moscow, to shake her hand and embrace her, instead of to this wretched dictator-ridden country where he was to deliver the Professor's rhetorical pages to a pro-Franco review. Meanwhile the train was taking him to Madrid. The journey was monotonous and the headquarters of the review disappointing, a colourless office in a building near the Prado, where a distracted employee thanked him in a perfunctory manner. Now Madrid was all his, even if he didn't take to it. He hated the aristocratic monumentality of the public buildings, the elegance of the fashionable section, the vastness of the Prado, the paradoxical, shapeless Goyas, all in the detestable styles of baroque monstrosity and romantic fantasy. He couldn't resist the temptation of taking a train across the Castilian plain, on a pilgrimage to Soria, a stripped, sober town to which he was drawn by a poem. The room in Doña Isabel Cuevas' boarding house was intact: a table, a chair, a bed, a washstand. He wandered with emotion through the unpretentious town, encircled by the lunar desert of Castile. In an antiquarian bookshop, he found, after considerable insistence, a photograph of Machado with a dedication in his own writing dated 22 January 1939, when the poet, hounded by Franco's police, was fleeing towards the frontier and death. The bookseller was a circumspect, suspicious fellow, fearful, perhaps, of a trap, and so, although his Castilian was first-rate, he spoke in Italian. His reassuring words obviously came from the heart; he held out the money and got what he wanted. Back in his Madrid hotel, a letter from the Professor awaited him, and it was in the terms of an obligation, an order laid upon him. He was to proceed to Lisbon on another errand; a first-class railway ticket was enclosed. Well, he was glad enough to go. The Professor wanted to place another of his stale articles in a Portuguese review, and he would take it there and make the necessary arrangements. Why not? It was almost a satisfaction, a sort of subtle revenge. The melancholy, honest face of Machado smiled at him from the bottom of his suitcase, he covered it with the Professor's pages and his personal belongings, took the train and, at the border, told the customs officer that he had nothing to declare. The slight risk that he was running was his revenge and his talisman.

In Lisbon they were polite and attentive, unlike the Spaniards. The review was located in a handsome building on the Placa dos Restauradores, the Palácio Foz, with an English-style façade, a slate roof, and heavily carpeted rooms. They sang the praises of the Professor and he went along with them, adding a more graceful and subtle appreciation of his own, whose slyness certainly escaped the pompous editor, an unconscious symbol of idiocy. Certainly, he said, with maximum hypocrisy, he too was a friend of Portugal, a small country but a great one. For the time being he couldn't contribute to the review; besides, his name meant nothing, he was only an assistant to the Professor and, moreover, he took no interest in politics. He might, eventually, be able to make some translations, under a fictitious name; his Portuguese wasn't all that good, but he could count on the help of a Portuguese reader in an Italian university, whom they doubtless knew. And they, in their turn, could count on his good will. The Professor was old, had many commitments and couldn't make frequent trips to Portugal. He, on the other hand, was happy to travel.

And so it went. The texts he was given to translate were

stupid and easy, but the pay was good. Their very stupidity
bore out his inner instincts, kindling the secret fire of his
resentment. As for the photograph of Machado, he hung it
over his table, between the bed and the window giving onto
the hospital courtyard. But he wouldn't be staying much
longer in this squalid rented room, he knew; a competitive
examination for a better post was in the offing. He would
come out first and then hang the photograph in a place
worthy of it. Meanwhile, half consciously, he was coming to
resemble his idol. He let his hair grow—bushy and unpom-
maded—over his forehead, giving it the shape of Machado's.
The cut of his mouth was similar also; the thin lips were like a
cynical slash, which dissembled the injustices to which he had
been subjected. He was reading the reflections attributed to
the fictitious Juan de Mairena and was fascinated by Machado's capacity to wear masks, by the subtle ability to assume
various roles, which he too enjoyed. "My philosophy is fun-
damentally sad, but I'm not a sad man, and I don't believe I
sadden anyone else. In other words, the fact that I don't put
my own philosophy into practice saves me from its evil spell,
or, rather, my faith in the human race is stronger than my
intellectual analysis of it; there lies the fountain of youth in
which my heart is continually bathing." *The fact that I don't
put my own philosophy into practice saves me from its evil
spell*—this notion gave him a feeling of infinite lightness, a
sort of remission of his pains, of innocence. It was in such a
state of innocence that he lived through the examination days
unaware of the difficulties involved. The examination was
not on Machado; obviously, it covered purely technical, theo-
retical matters of metrics. And yet this very abstract poetical
grammar, so proudly uncontaminated, seemed to him a metaphor of his existence, of pure thought, free of thought's harmful effects. He passed the examination with flying colours,
just as he had expected. And, at this point, it was easy, too easy
to give him any satisfaction, to cast off the old Professor.

When he took him the second edition of his thesis, minus the hateful dedication, he felt that he was carrying out an insipid and disappointing obligation. If the Professor had been argumentative, if he had lashed out against him, as he had expected, there would have been a frank, excited discussion. The Professor was waiting for him in his study with a melancholy air; he played the part of a man betrayed and shunted aside and welcomed him with tears in his eyes and no courage to put up a fight. "I didn't know that you were my enemy," he said; "it's the greatest sorrow of my old age." It was sentimental blackmail, based on a presumed friendship, old age, and disillusionment, which reminded him of Cecilia's oblique reproaches. And he couldn't bear this because it was a subtle and yet unfair way to recall Madrid and Lisbon, to accuse him of that silent and bitter scorn of which he had undoubtedly been aware and with which the Professor now hoped to put pressure upon him. At this point he voiced his disdain, calmly but sarcastically, in sentences whose rhythm recalled the Machado of the *Coplas per la muerte di don Guido*. While he whispered bare, cutting words of revenge, his mind, off on its own tack, freed by thought from thought's harmful effects, silently recited, in a familiar rhythm: *Al fin, una pulmonia mató a don Guido, y están las campans todo el día doblando por el: din-dan! Murió don Guido, un señor de mozo muy jaranero, muy galán e algo torero, de viejo, gran rezador.* ". . . This was the death of Don Guido, a gentleman who, when young, was very haughty, very gallant and something of a bullfighter; but when old was given to prayer." The Professor interrupted his silent recital and told him to go away, and he went, savouring the taste of victory. For it *was* a victory, and he knew that many other victories were to follow.

The second was Giuliana, a victory not over her but over life. He rescued her from the status of a premature old maid and restored to her a youthfulness that she tried to conceal, erasing her idea that she was ill and replacing it with the

conviction that she was healthy, all too healthy, and needed
only a man to give her protection and a feeling of security.
The only thing about her that disturbed him was her conciliatory nature, of a transparency which seemed to him simple-
minded and perhaps damaging to them both. He made her do
away with violet perfume, a modest lambswool coat, loud
laughter, and anything else that might make her conspicuous.
He would teach her or, rather, "construct" for her the pattern
of a university career, which was to be learned like a profession. This didn't mean that she was to be his creature, that
would be an oversimplified interpretation. What they had was
a common purpose, an existential partnership, that was his
idea of love, if only she could understand. And she understood.

Other victories came in a pleasing enough manner. Chiefly
victory over a colleague who thoughtlessly or frivolously had
wronged him. Such wrongs are searing because they pre-
suppose a lack of attention to the wronged party. And he
could not tolerate inattentiveness, it was a form of humilia-
tion that made him pale, one which he had experienced all
too many times, which reminded him of the days when he was
a pariah, when he had had to buy wretched suits at the shop on
the Viale Libia and to imagine that they were well-tailored.
But searing wrongs are the richest and most productive; they
swell in the mind and postulate elaborate and complex
answers, not rapid and disappointing acts of liberation. No,
he knew that searing wrongs nest in some secret area; they
crouch there like lethargic larvae and then create ramifica-
tions, colonies, anthills with winding passageways which
deserve their own painstaking, detailed topography. A topography which he had studied in painstaking detail, patiently,
because there was no way of taking direct revenge except
through an unsatisfactory, poisonously personal attack in
some scholarly periodical. He had, then, to find an indirect

approach. This called for alliances, deliciously allusive con-
versations, subtle understandings, elective affinities.

There is a delicate pleasure in identifying the friends of our
enemies and making them the secret objectives of revenge. He
worked on it for months, years. His enemy's favourite student
had just gone to a university in the north; by one of life's little
coincidences he was in the same field. To find a possible
enemy for him was difficult but not impossible; he had only
to study the location of various colleagues and the second one
he found was a good choice. He didn't know the man well.
He'd met him at some congress or other and was on first name
terms. He was a mediocre, arrogant fellow whose writings
were marked by awkward syntax and vague conclusions; they
extolled second-rate authors in second-rate reviews. But this
was not his Achilles' heel. The weak point of this prospective
ally was his wearisome career in the shadow of a pitiless
superior who had humiliated him for years as if he were a
superfluous object, calling him Smerdyakov, like the servant
of the Brothers Karamazov. Here was the weakness to be
exploited, not heavy-handedly but with a light touch, which
would not threaten blackmail but surreptitiously hint at it in
a way possible between congenial spirits. After only a brief
conversation the machinery was put in motion and he
watched it from the sidelines with deliberately prolonged
enjoyment. An enjoyment which followed a set course to the
very end, like a symphony. And when it was over he started
again and finished with a short, syncopated rondo, which was
easier but less gratifying. His second alliance, with an ambi-
tious and spiteful young woman colleague gave him little
satisfaction. She was a frank and obvious schemer who had
betrayed a friend, usurped her place with the old Professor
and installed herself, almost insolently in his department. To
have her on his side was actually tedious; privately he called
her "the gangster's moll".

And the other victories, the official ones. Published books, articles, scholarly meetings. His greatest success came, once more, from the Iberian Peninsula. The dictatorships were over, there were no more limitations, and no one to prevent him from exercising his critical powers on a sixteenth-century courtier-poet, commemorated at a congress of scholars from all over Europe which took place in an aristocratic, baroque country mansion, far from the capital and surrounded by olive trees and vineyards. He had managed to be scheduled near the end, intending to deliver a dry, technical paper, an apparently neutral, rhythmical reading which actually pointed up relentlessly the stylistic wiles of the poet in question, his concealed plagiarism of his great contemporaries. But at one point there was a paper by a Dominican monk, of his own age, a professor of Classics and for years editor of a literary review which, during the superseded government had held to a vaguely liberal and anti-Fascist "cultural" line, with no definite political colouring. Now this champion of vague anti-Fascism spoke in a conciliatory manner of the compromising courtier-poet, in terms of the autonomy of the poetical text, of human weakness and the necessity of putting aside biographical details, because "poets have no biography except in their poetry", and we must pay due respect to the solitary, mysterious inner Word which dictated the words of their poems. There was intolerable Platonism in this specious and surreptitious allusion, a fuzziness that spilled over into a metaphysical *logos,* an influence of Spinoza which the speaker gracefully linked with pre-Socratic philosophy but which was actually tied up with Right-wing neo-idealism. And then the monk's humility, his conciliatory tone, his forgiveness of human weakness in the name of the poetic text, these were a form of subtle arrogance, a reversed censorship, a blackmailing expression of the remission of sins. No, no sin was to be remitted; he would not tolerate such a vision of the world or let himself be trapped by so treacherous a formula.

And so he spoke up as he thought he should under the circumstances. First he apologized for quoting himself, he simply had to do it. Meanwhile he called his hearers' attention to examples of phonetics, scansion, and vocabulary which he had picked out in order to show the similarities between the poet's text and those of his manneristic contemporaries. He was perfectly aware of the autonomy of a poetical text, but every text has its place in a context, and the context was here. At this point he unsheathed his long sword. The classicist had used old-fashioned, outdated language—he was not up on contemporary criticism; in short, he was poorly equipped. And so he spoke of Bachtin and the meaning of context within the text; he displayed the gems of his chosen examples against a broad cultural panorama. This allowed for no indulgence or compromise; he left no space for the no-man's-land of literature shaped by a Platonic canon; he showed them, peremptorily and incontrovertibly, an x-ray labelled literature and life. And he won. Not immediately, of course, because he incurred an aggressive attack on the part of three young intellectuals. But the important thing was that in academic circles he won the reputation of an uncompromising scholar, with a cutting edge like that of a diamond.

And then there were comforting and reassuring domestic victories: an apartment in the centre of the city, a rich library, a study where the photograph of Machado was finally hung in an appropriate setting, near to books that were worthy of him. He transcribed the tercet of the curious poem by Drummond de Andrade that he had chosen to analyze, and wondered what title to give to its presentation at a forthcoming congress. He attempted a translation and read it aloud in order to measure the effect it would have on his hearers.

> *What are our poems made of? And where?*
> *What poisoned dream responds to them*
> *If the poet is embittered and the rest is clouds?*

He rather liked the poet, after all; he was dry and realistic, with clear vision, even if it was, perhaps, veiled by a metaphysical streak which he considered superfluous. On second thoughts there was something querulous in that late-Romantic reference to a vague empyrean where poetical concepts floated in abstract form before descending in the shape of words into such a miserable receptacle as the poet, a mortal man contaminated by sin and embitterment. But perhaps this elegantly melancholy poet was unaware; he was, in his way, a young gentleman who had written these words without understanding their meaning, in the belief that they had mysteriously arisen out of some depth of cosmic space. But for him, as he read them, they held no mystery, they were clear as crystal, he had the key, he could snatch and hold them in the palm of his hand, and play with them as if they were the wooden letters of a child's alphabet. He smiled and wrote: *Bitterness and Clouds. For a rhythmical reading of a twentieth-century poem.*

He himself was the true poet, he could feel it.

ISLANDS

He thought he might put it this way: Dear Maria Assunta, I am well and hope the same is true of you. Here it's already hot, it's nearly summer, but with you, on the other hand, good weather perhaps hasn't yet come; we're always hearing about smog, and then there's all that big-city and industrial waste. Anyhow I'm expecting you if you want to come for a holiday, with Giannandrea, too, of course, and God bless you. I want to thank you for his and your invitation, but I've decided not to come, because, you know, your mother and I lived here together for thirty-five years. When we first came we felt as if we were in the North, and in fact we were, but now I've grown fond of the place and it's filled with memories. Then, since your mother's death I've grown accustomed to living alone and even if I miss my work I can find a lot of distractions, like looking after the garden, something I've always enjoyed doing, and also after the two blackbirds, which keep me company, too, and what would I do in a big city, and so I've decided to stay in these four rooms, where I can see the harbour and if I feel like it I can take the ferry to go and visit my old mates and have a game of cards. It's only a few hours by ferry, and I feel at home on board, because a man misses the place where he has worked all his life, every week for a lifetime.

He peeled the orange, dropped the peel into the water, watched it float in the foaming wake of the boat and imagined that he had finished one page and was starting another, because he simply had to say that he was missing his work already; it was his last day of service and already he missed it. Missed what? A lifetime aboard the boat, the trip out and the trip in, I don't know whether you remember, Maria Assunta, you were very little and your mother used to say: how is this little one ever going to become a big girl? I got up early; in winter it was still dark and I gave you a kiss before going out; it was bitterly cold and they never gave us decent coats, only old horse-blankets dyed blue, those were our uniforms. All those years made for a habit, and I ask you again what would I do in a big city, what would I do in your house at five o'clock in the morning? I can't stay in bed any later; I get up at five, as I did for forty years, it's as if an alarm clock rang inside me. And then you've had schooling and school changes people even if they're from the same background; and the same with your husband—what would we have to talk about? He has ideas, which can't be mine, from this point of view we don't exactly get along. You're educated, both of you; that time when I came with your mother and after dinner some friends of yours arrived, I didn't say a word the whole evening. All I could talk about were things I knew, that I learned in the course of my life, and you'd asked me not to mention my job. Then there's something else, which may seem silly to you, who knows how Giannandrea would laugh, but I couldn't live with the furniture in your house. It's all glass, and I bump into it because I don't see it. So many years, you understand, with my own furniture and getting up at five o'clock.

But, mentally, he crumpled up this last page, just as he had written it and threw it into the sea where he imagined he could see it floating, together with the orange peel.

— 2 —

"I sent for you so that you'd take off the handcuffs," the man said in a low voice.

His shirt was unbuttoned and his eyes were closed as if he were sleeping. He seemed to have a yellow complexion, but perhaps it was the curtain strung across the porthole that gave the whole cabin this colour. How old could he be; thirty, thirty-five? Perhaps no older than Maria Assunta; prison ages a man quickly. And then that emaciated look. He felt a sudden curiosity and thought to ask the fellow his age. He took off his hat and sat down on the opposite bunk. The man had opened his eyes and was looking at him. The eyes were blue and, who knows why, this touched his feelings. "How old are you?" he asked in a formal manner. Formal, perhaps because this was the end of his service. And the man was a political prisoner, which was something special. Now he sat up and looked at him hard out of his big blue eyes. He had a blond moustache and ruffled hair. He was young, yes, younger than he seemed. "I told you to take off my hand-cuffs," he said, in a weary voice. "I want to write a letter, and my arms hurt." The accent was from the North, but he didn't know one northern accent from another. Piedmontese, per-haps. "Are you afraid I'll escape?" he asked ironically. "Look here, I won't run away, I won't attack you, I won't do any-thing. I wouldn't have the strength." He pressed one hand against his stomach, with a quick smile which traced two deep furrows in his cheeks. "And then it's my last trip," he added.

When the handcuffs were off he poked about in a small canvas bag, taking out a comb, a pen and a yellow notebook. "If you don't mind I'd rather be alone to write," he said; "your presence bothers me. I'd appreciate it if you'd wait outside the cabin. If you're afraid I may do something you can stay by the door. I promise not to make trouble."

— 3 —

And then he'd surely find something to do. When you've
work you're not so alone. But real work, which would yield
not only satisfaction but also money. Chinchillas, for instance. In theory he already knew all about them. A prisoner
who had raised them before his arrest had told him. They're
charming little creatures; just don't let them bite your hands.
They're tough and adaptable, they reproduce even in places
where there isn't much light. Perhaps the closet in the cellar
would do, if the landlord would allow it. The man on the
second floor kept hamsters.

He leaned against the rail and loosened his shirt collar.
Hardly nine o'clock and it was already hot. It was the first day
of real summer heat. He fancied he smelled scorched earth and
with the smell came the picture of a country road running
among prickly pear plants, where a barefoot boy walked towards a house with a lemon tree: his childhood. He took
another orange from the bag he had bought the evening
before and began to peel it. The price was impossibly high at
this season, but he had allowed himself a treat. He threw the
peel into the sea and caught a glimpse of the shining coast.
Currents outlined bright strips in the water, like the wake of
other ships. Quickly he calculated the time. The prison guard
would be waiting at the pier and the formality of turning the
prisoner over to him would take a quarter of an hour. He
could reach the barracks towards noon; it wasn't far. He
fingered the inside pocket of his jacket to check that his
discharge papers were there. If he were lucky enough to find
the sergeant in the barracks he'd have finished by one o'clock.
And by half-past one he'd be sitting under the pergola of the
restaurant at the far end of the harbour. He knew the place
well but he'd never eaten there. Whenever he passed by he
paused to look at the menu displayed on a sign surmounted
by a swordfish painted in metallic blue. He had an empty

feeling in his stomach, but it couldn't be hunger. At any rate
he let his imagination play over the dishes listed on the sign.
Today it will be fish soup and red mullet, he said to himself,
and fried zucchini, if he chose. To top it off, a fruit cup or,
better still, cherries. And a cup of coffee. Then he'd ask for a
sheet of paper and an envelope and spend the afternoon writing the letter. Because you see, Maria Assunta, when you work
you're not so alone, but it must be real work, which yields not
only satisfaction but also a bit of money. And so I've decided
to raise chinchillas, they're charming creatures as long as you
don't let them bite your hands. They're tough and adaptable
and they reproduce even in places where there isn't much
light. But in your house it would be impossible, you can see
that, Maria Assunta, not because of Giannandrea, whom I
respect even if we don't have the same ideas; it's a question of
space and here I have the cellar closet. It may not be ideal, but
if the man on the floor above me raises hamsters in a closet I
don't see why I can't do the same thing.

A voice from behind caused him to start. "Officer, the
prisoner wants to see you."

— 4 —

The guard was a lanky fellow with a pimpled face and long
arms sticking out below sleeves that were too short. He wore
his uniform awkwardly and spoke the way he had been
trained to. "He didn't say why," he added.

He told the guard to take his place on deck and went down
the stairs leading to the cabins. As he crossed the saloon he
saw the captain chatting with a passenger at the bar. For years
he'd seen him there and now he waved his hand in a gesture
that was less a greeting than a sign of old acquaintance. He
slowed his pace wanting to tell the captain that he wouldn't
see him that evening: it's my last day of service and tonight I'll
stay on the mainland, where I have some things to attend to.

Then it suddenly seemed ridiculous. He went down the next flight of stairs to the cabin deck, then along the bare, clean passageway, taking the master-key off his chain. The prisoner was standing near the porthole, looking out to sea. He wheeled around and looked at him out of those childlike blue eyes. "I want to give you this letter," he said. He had an envelope in his hand and held it out with a timid but at the same time peremptory gesture. "Take it," he said; "I want you to post it for me." He had buttoned up his shirt and combed his hair and his face was not as haggard as before. "Do you realize what you're asking?" he answered. "You know quite well I can't do it."

The prisoner sat down on the bed and looked at him in a manner that seemed ironical, or perhaps it was just his child-like eyes. "Of course you can do it," he said, "if you want to." He had unpacked his canvas bag and lined up the contents on his bunk as if he were making an inventory. "I know what's wrong with me," he said. "Look at my hospital admission card, have a look. Do you know what it means? It means I'll never get out of that hospital. This is a last trip, do you follow me?" He emphasized the word "last" with an odd intonation, as if it were a joke. He paused as if to catch his breath and once more pressed his hand against his stomach, nervously or as if in pain. "This letter is for someone very dear to me and, for reasons I'm not going to bother explaining, I don't want it to be censored. Just try to understand, I know you do." The ship's siren sounded as it always did when the harbour was in sight. It was a happy sound, something like a snort.

He answered angrily, in a hard, perhaps too hard voice, but there was no other way to end the conversation. "Repack your bag," he said hurriedly, trying not to look him in the eyes. "In half an hour we'll be there. I'll come back when we land to put your handcuffs in place." That was the expression he used: put them in place.

— 5 —

In a matter of seconds the few passangers dispersed and the pier was empty. An enormous yellow crane moved across the sky towards buildings under construction, with blind windows. The construction yard siren whistled, signalling that work should stop and a church bell in the town made a reply. It was noon. Who knows why the mooring operation had taken so long? The houses along the waterfront were red and yellow; he reflected that he'd never really noticed them and looked more closely. He sat down on an iron stanchion with a rope from a boat wound around it. It was hot, and he took off his cap. Then he started to walk along the pier in the direction of the crane. The usual old dog, with his head between his paws, lay in front of the combined bar and tobacco shop and wagged his tail feebly as he went by. Four boys in T-shirts, near the juke-box, were joking loudly. A hoarse, slightly masculine woman's voice carried him back across the years. She was singing *Ramona* and he thought it was strange that this song should have come back into fashion. Summer was really here.

The restaurant at the far end of the harbour was not yet open. The owner, wearing a white apron, with a sponge in hand, was wiping a deposit of salt and sand from the shutters. The fellow looked at him and smiled in recognition, the way we smile at people we've known for most of our life but for whom we have no feelings. He smiled back and walked on, turning into a street with abandoned railway tracks, which he followed to the freight yard. At the end of one of the platforms there was a letterbox whose red paint was eaten by rust. He read the hour of the next collection: five o'clock. He didn't want to know where the letter was going but he was curious about the name of the person who would receive it, only the Christian name. He carefully covered the address with his hand and looked only at the name: Lisa. She was called Lisa. Strange, it occurred to him: he knew the name of the recipient without knowing her, and he knew the sender without knowing his name. He didn't remember it because there's no reason to remember the name of a prisoner. He slipped the letter into the box and turned around to look back at the sea. The sunlight was strong and the gleam on the horizon hid the points of the islands. He felt perspiration on his face and took off his cap in order to wipe his forehead. My name's Nicola, he said aloud. There was no one anywhere near.

THE TRAINS THAT GO
TO MADRAS

The trains from Bombay to Madras leave from Victoria Station. My guide assured me that a departure from Victoria Station was, of itself, as good as a trip through India, and this was my first reason for taking the train rather than a plane. My guide was an eccentric little book, which gave utterly incongruous advice, and I followed it to the letter. My whole trip was incongruous and so this guidebook suited me to perfection. It treated the traveller not like an avid collector of stereotype images to be visited, as in a museum, by three or four set itineraries, but like a footloose and illogical individual, disposed to taking it easy and making mistakes. By plane, it said, you'll have a fast, comfortable trip but you'll miss out on the India of unforgettable villages and countrysides. With long-distance trains you risk unscheduled stops and may arrive as much as a whole day late, but you'll see the true India. If you have the luck to hit the right train it will be not only comfortable but on time as well; you'll enjoy first-rate food and service and spend only half as much as you would on a plane. And don't forget that on Indian trains you may make the most unexpected acquaintances.

These last points had definitely convinced me, and perhaps I was so lucky as to have hit the right train. We had crossed strikingly beautiful country, unforgettable, also, for the variety of its human components, the air-conditioning worked perfectly and the service was faultless. Dusk was falling as the train crossed an area of bare red mountains. The steward came in with tea on a lacquered tray, gave me a dampened towel, poured the tea and informed me, discreetly, that we were in the centre of the country. While I was eating he made up my berth and told me that the dining-car would be open until midnight and that, if I wanted to dine in my own compartment, I had only to ring the bell. I thanked him with a small tip and gave him back the tray. Then I smoked a cigarette, looking out of the window at the unfamiliar landscape and wondering about my strange itinerary. For an agnostic to go to Madras to visit the Theosophical Society, and to spend the better part of two days on the train to get there was an undertaking that would probably have pleased the unusual authors of my unusual guidebook. The fact was that a member of the Theosophical Society might be able to tell me something I very much wanted to know. It was a slender hope, perhaps an illusion, and I didn't want to consume it in the short space of a plane flight; I preferred to cradle and savour it in a leisurely fashion, as we like to do with hopes that we cherish while knowing that there is little chance of their realization.

An abrupt braking of the train intruded on my thoughts and probably my torpor. I must have dozed off for a few minutes while the train was entering a station and I had no time to read the sign displaying the name of the place. I had read in the guidebook that one of the stops was at Mangalore, or perhaps Bangalore, I couldn't remember which, but now I didn't want to bother leafing through the book to trace the railway line. Waiting on the platform there were some apparently prosperous Indian travellers in western dress, a group of women and a flurry of porters. It must have been an important industrial city; in the distance, beyond the tracks, there were factory smokestacks, tall buildings and broad, tree-lined avenues.

The man came in while the train was just starting to move again. He greeted me hastily, matched the number on his ticket with that of the berth and, after he had found that they tallied, apologized for his intrusion. He was a portly, bulging European, wearing a dark-blue suit, quite inappropriate to the climate, and a fine hat. His luggage consisted of a black leather overnight bag. He sat down, pulled a white handkerchief out of his pocket and, with a smile on his face, proceeded to clean his glasses. He had an affable, almost apologetic air. "Are you going to Madras too?" he asked, and added, without waiting for an answer, "This train is highly reliable. We'll be there at seven o'clock in the morning."

He spoke good English, with a German accent, but he didn't look like a German. Dutch, I thought to myself, for no particular reason, or Swiss. He looked like a businessman, around sixty years of age, perhaps a bit older. "Madras is the capital of Dravidian India," he went on. "If you've never been there you'll see extraordinary things." He spoke in the detached, casual manner of someone well-acquainted with the country, and I prepared myself for a string of platitudes. I thought it a good idea to tell him that we could still go to the dining-car, where the probable banality of his conversation would be interrupted by the silent manipulations of knife and fork demanded by good table manners.

As we walked through the corridor I introduced myself, apologizing for not having done so before. "Oh, introductions have become useless formalities," he said with his affable air. And, slightly inclining his head, he added: "My name's Peter."

On the subject of dinner he revealed himself to be an expert. He advised me against the vegetable chops which, out of sheer curiosity, I was considering, "because the vegetables have to be very varied and carefully worked over," he said, "and that's not likely to be the case aboard a train." Timidly I proposed some other dishes, purely random selections, all of which he disapproved. Finally I agreed to take the lamb *tandoori*, which he had chosen for himself, "because the lamb is a noble, sacrificial animal, and Indians have a feeling for the ritual quality of food."

We talked at length about Dravidian civilization, that is, he talked, and I confined myself to a few typically ignorant questions and an occasional feeble objection. He described, with a wealth of details, the cliff reliefs of Kancheepuram, and the architecture of the Shore Temple; he spoke of unknown, archaic cults extraneous to Hindu pantheism, of the significance of colours and castes and funeral rites. Hesitantly I brought up my own lore: the legend of the martyrdom of Saint Thomas at Madras, the French presence at Pondicherry, the European penetration of the coasts of Tamil, the unsuccessful attempt of the Portuguese to found another Goa in the same area and their wars with the local potentates. He rounded out my notions and corrected my inexactness in regard to indigenous dynasties, spelling out names, places, dates and events. He spoke with competence and assurance; his vast erudition seemed to mark him as an expert, perhaps a university professor or, in any case, a serious scholar. I put the question to him, frankly and with a certain ingenuousness, sure that he would make an affirmative answer. He smiled, with a certain false modesty, and shook his head. "I'm only an amateur," he said. "I've a passion that fate has spurred me to cultivate."

There was a note of distress in his voice, I thought, expressive of regret or sorrow. His eyes glistened, and his smooth face seemed paler under the lights of the dining-car. His hands were delicate and his gestures weary. His whole bearing had something incomplete and indefinable about it, a sort of hidden sickliness or shame.

We returned to our compartment and went on talking, but his liveliness had subsided and our conversation was punctuated by long silences. While we were getting ready for bed I asked him, for no specific reason, why he was travelling by train instead of by plane. I thought that, at his age, it would have been easier and more comfortable to take a plane rather than undergo so long a journey. I expected that his answer would be a confession of fear of air travel, shared by people who have not been accustomed to it from an early age.

He looked at me with perplexity, as if such a thing had never occurred to him. Then, suddenly, his face lit up and he said: "By plane you have a fast and comfortable trip, but you miss out on the real India. With long-distance trains you risk arriving as much as a day late, but if you hit the right one you'll be just as comfortable and arrive on time. And on a train there's always the pleasure of a conversation that you'd never have in the air."

Unable to hold myself back, I murmured, *"India, A Travel Survival Kit."*

"What's that?"

"Nothing," I said. "I was thinking of a book." And I added, boldly, "You've never been to Madras."

He looked at me ingenuously. "You can know a place without ever having been there." He took off his jacket and shoes, put his overnight bag under the pillow, pulled the curtain of his berth, and said goodnight.

I should have liked to say that he, too, had taken the train because he cherished a slender hope and preferred to cradle and savour it rather than consume it in the short space of a plane flight. I was sure of it. But, of course, I said nothing. I turned off the overhead light, leaving the blue night-lamp lit, pulled my curtain and said only goodnight.

*   *   *

We were awakened by someone's turning on the ceiling light and speaking in a loud voice. Just outside our window there was a wooden structure, lit by a dim lamp and bearing an incomprehensible sign. The train conductor was accompanied by a dark-skinned policeman with a suspicious air. "We're in Tamil Nadu," said the conductor, smiling; "this is a mere formality." The policeman held out his hand: "Your papers, please."

He looked distractedly at my passport and quickly shut it, but lingered longer over my companion's. While he was examining it I noticed that it came from Israel. "Mr. . . . Shi . . . mail?" he asked, pronouncing the name with difficulty.

"Schlemihl," the Israeli corrected him. "Peter Schlemihl."

The policeman gave us back our passports, nodded coolly and put out the light. The train was running again through the Indian night and the blue night-lamp created a dreamlike atmosphere. For a long time we were silent, then I said: "You can't have a name like that. There's only one Peter Schlemihl, the shadowless man, he's a creation of Chamisso, as you know very well. You could pass it off on an Indian policeman, of course . . ."

He did not reply for a minute. Then he asked, "Do you like Thomas Mann?"

"Not all of him," I answered.

"What, then?"

"The stories. Some of the short novels. *Tonio Kröger, Death in Venice.*"

"I wonder if you know the preface to Chamisso's *Peter Schlemihl*," he said. "An admirable piece of writing."

Again there was silence between us. I thought he might have fallen asleep. But no, he couldn't have. He was waiting for me to speak, and I did.

"What are you doing in Madras?"

He did not answer at once, but coughed slightly. "I'm going to see a statue," he murmured.

"A long trip just to see a statue."

He did not reply, but blew his nose several times in succession. "I want to tell you a little story," he said at last. "I want to tell you a little story." He was speaking softly, and his voice was dulled by the curtain. "Many years ago, in Germany, I ran across a man, a doctor, whose job it was to give me a physical examination. He sat behind a desk and I stood, naked, before him. Behind me there was a line of other naked men waiting to be examined. When we were taken to that place we were told that we were useful to the cause of German science. Beside the doctor there were two armed guards, and a nurse who was filling out cards. The doctor asked us very precise questions about the functioning of our male organs; the nurse made some measurements which she then wrote down. The line was moving fast because the doctor was in a hurry. When my turn was over, instead of moving on to the next room where we were to go, I lingered for a few seconds to look at a statuette on the doctor's desk which had caught my attention. It represented an oriental deity, one I had never seen, a dancing figure with the arms and legs harmoniously diverging within a circle. In the circle there were not many empty spaces, only a few openings waiting to be closed by the imagination of the viewer. The doctor became aware of my fascination and smiled. He had a tight-lipped, mocking mouth. 'This statue,' he said, 'represents the vital circle into which all waste matter must enter in order to attain that superior form of life which is beauty. I hope that in the biological cycle envisaged by the philosophy which conceived of this statue you may attain, in another life, a place higher than the one you occupy in this one.'"

At this point my companion halted. In spite of the sound made by the train I could hear his deep, regular breathing.

"Please go on," I said.

"There's not much more to say. The statuette was a dancing Shiva, but that I didn't know. As you see, I haven't yet entered the recycling circle, and my own interpretation of the figure is a different one. I've thought of it every day of my life since then; indeed, it's the only thing I've thought of in all these years."

"How many years has it been?"

"Forty."

"Can you think of one thing only for forty years?"

"Yes, I think so, if you've been subjected to indignity."

"And what is your interpretation of the figure?"

"I don't think it represents a vital circle. It's simply the dance of life."

"And how is that different?"

"Oh, it's very different," he murmured. "Life is a circle. One day the circle must close, and we don't know what day that will be." He blew his nose again and said, "Excuse me, please; I'm tired and should like to catch a bit of sleep."

*   *   *

When I woke up we were drawing near to Madras. My travelling companion was already shaved and fully dressed in his impeccable dark-blue suit. He had pushed up his berth and now, looking thoroughly rested and with a smile on his face, he pointed to the breakfast tray on the table next to the window.

"I waited for you to wake up so that we could drink our tea together," he said. "You were so fast asleep that I didn't want to disturb you."

I went into the washroom and made my morning toilet, gathered my belongings together and closed my suitcase, then sat down to breakfast. We were running through an area of clustered villages, with the first signs of the approaching city.

"As you see, we're right on time," he said. "It's exactly a quarter to seven." Then, folding his napkin, he added: "I wish you'd go to see that statue. It's in the museum. And I'd like to hear what you think of it." He got up, reached for his bag, held out his other hand and bade me goodbye. "I'm grateful to my guidebook for the choice of the best means of transportation. It's true that on Indian trains you may make the most unexpected acquaintances. Your company has given me pleasure and solace."

"It's been a mutual pleasure," I answered. "I'm the one who's grateful to the guidebook."

We were entering the station, alongside a crowded platform. The train's brakes went on and we glided to a stop. I stepped aside and he got off first, waving his hand. As he started to walk away I called out to him.

"I don't know where to send my reaction to the statue. I haven't your address."

He wheeled about, with the perplexed expression I had seen on his face before. After a moment's reflection, he said: "Leave me a message at the American Express. I'll pick it up."

Then we went our separate ways among the crowd.

*   *   *

I stayed only three days in Madras, intense, almost feverish days. Madras is an enormous agglomeration of low buildings and immense uncultivated spaces, jammed with bicycles, animals, and random buses; getting from one end of the city to another required a very long time. After I had fulfilled my obligations I had only one free day and I chose to go, not to the museum but to the cliff reliefs of Kancheepuram, some miles from the city. Here, too, my guidebook was a precious companion.

On the morning of the fourth day I was at the depot for buses to Kerala and Goa. There was an hour before departure

time, it was scorchingly hot and the shade of the roofed
platforms afforded the only relief from the heat. In order to
while away the time I bought the English-language newspaper, a four-page sheet that looked like a parish bulletin,
containing local news, summaries of popular films, notices,
and advertisements of every kind. Prominently displayed on
the front page there was the story of a murder committed the
day before. The victim was an Argentinian citizen who had
been living in Madras since 1958. He was described as a
discreet, retiring gentleman in his seventies, without close
friends, who had a house in the residential section of Adyar.
His wife had died three years before, from natural causes.
They had no children.

He had been killed with a pistol shot to the heart. The
murder defied explanation, since no theft was involved: everything in the house was in order and there was no sign that
anything had been broken into. The article described the
house as simple and sober, possessing a few well-chosen art
objects and with a small garden around it. It seemed that the
victim was a connoisseur of Dravidian art; he had taken part
in the cataloguing of the Dravidian section of the local museum. His photograph showed a bald old man with blue eyes
and thin lips. The report of the episode was bland and factual.
The only interesting detail was the photograph of a statuette,
alongside that of the victim. A logical juxtaposition, since he
was an expert on Dravidian art, and the Dance of Shiva is the
best known work in the Madras museum, and a sort of symbol
as well. But this logical juxtaposition caused me to connect
one thing with another. There were twenty minutes left before
the departure of my bus; I looked for a telephone and dialled
the number of the American Express, where a young woman
answered politely. "I'd like to leave a message for Mr. Schlemihl," I told her. The girl asked me to wait a minute and then
said, "At the moment we've no such name on record, but you

can leave your message all the same, if you like, and it will be delivered to him when he comes by."

"Hello, hello!" she repeated when she did not hear any reply.

"Just a minute, operator," I said; "let me think."

What was I to say. My message had a ridiculous side. Perhaps I had understood something. But exactly what? That, for someone, the circle had closed?

"It doesn't matter," I said; "I've changed my mind." And I hung up.

*   *   *

I don't deny that my imagination may have been working overtime. But if I guessed correctly what shadow Peter Schlemihl, like Chamisso's hero, had lost, and if he ever happens, by the same strange chance that brought about our meeting on the train, to read this story, I'd like to convey my greetings. And my sorrow.

SLEIGHT OF HAND

Because, at bottom, habit is a rite; we think we're doing something for our pleasure but actually we're carrying out a duty that we've imposed upon ourselves. Or else, it's a charm, he reflected, perhaps habit is a kind of exorcism, and then we feel it as a pleasure. Was it really a pleasure to take the ferry from the Battery, that Saturday, among the crowd of dazed tourists, to make the crossing, which inevitably gave him a squeamish feeling in his stomach, to walk around the enormous granite pedestal and look at seagulls and skyscrapers? No, no pleasure, he admitted to himself, or, rather, no longer a pleasure. It was a rite, obviously in remembrance of an excursion made for the first time years ago when Dolores was still there. We had looked up at the enormous bulk of Liberty, holding out her torch like a promise. To whom, and for when? Then it had a different meaning, it was a pilgrimage and at the same time a talisman, a send-off for the first transaction. Perhaps now it was for Dolores, he was doing it for her, in her memory; it was a continual, repetitive action, like that of a man who refuses to change his habits for fear of obliterating a memory. For the same reason he liked to take the subway to Brooklyn Heights, to wander around streets lined with decaying nineteenth-century houses. He could still hear her voice and the typically South American double s sound when she spoke of her devotion to "La Ca*uss*a." Like "Ro*ss*ario", for "Rosario" the ice-cream parlour in Little Italy, which was also part of the rite, a tribute to times gone by. Dolores liked Italians, more than he did in spite of his Sicilian mother. The old proprietor had died two years ago, now the place was run by his American-ized son, there was no one he knew, only anonymous faces; a pistachio ice-cream and a glass of club soda, please. He and Dolores used to sit in a booth in one corner; the partition had a panel of black leather bearing a framed view of Mount Etna. Tired. Yes, he was tired. *La Causa*, an evening at the Opera. What a bright idea! Every now and then *they* had these ideas. He'd have liked, just once, to meet *them*. Where were they, anyhow? New York, London, Geneva, where? They managed the money and transmitted orders, in a clean, efficient, silent manner, from far away. A post-office box, an assumed name, come in once a month, sometimes months with nothing to do, absolutely nothing, silence, sometimes a ticket like this one, from one day to the next. "The Met, Sunday, 2 November, fourth row orchestra, Rigoletto, Scene 7, deliver at *Sparafucil mi nomino*, take the usual rake-off, VIVA LA CAUSA." That was all, together with the ticket for the first seat on the fourth row, whence the entire row could be surveyed with only a slight inclination of the head. Idiots. "For the rest, try to take care of it yourself." The rest was quite a lot. He went to the toilets, stopping on the way at the pay phone to call Bolívar. There was an infernal noise in the workshop, but that didn't matter; the conversation was brief: "Do you have it?" "Yes, I have it." "I'll be right there." "I'll expect you." He didn't hang up right away, which was breaking the rules, he knew, but he was furious; those idiots are sending me to the Opera, they're playing at James Bond. When he hung up it was abruptly, as if the telephone were to blame.

And now all the rest. First of all the hotel, that hotel called

. . . what *was* it called; he'd passed in front of it so many times and still the name wouldn't come. Old age, that was why. The devil with old age, stupid old man, it's those idiots who've lapsed into second childhood with their silly games! Better try Tourist Information. "Hello, Miss, I'd like the names of three or four hotels near to Central Park, the best, mind you, and their telephone numbers." "Just a second." A few hundred seconds! Rosario Jr. was signalling from the counter that the pistachio ice-cream was melting. "Yes, you can tell me, I'm writing them down. Plaza, Pierre, Mayfair, Ritz Carlton, Park Lane, . . . that's enough, thank you." I may as well make the calls, the ice-cream has completely melted. Rosario Jr. can only throw it away. No rooms at the Plaza, of course, this city is full of millionaires, same thing at the Pierre. Nice if there were something at the Mayfair, where there's a first-class restaurant, Le Cirque: he'd been there before so he knew he could count on a good midnight supper after the Opera. "See if you can't find a room for me, it's only for one night." "Sorry, sir, everything's taken, nothing I can do." Devil take you then. The Park Lane, at last, there had to be a room in those forty-six storeys. "Yes, I'll hold it for you, Mr. Franklin. Good evening and thank you." He was worn out. But now it was done; time enough to call for the parcel tomorrow, better not keep all that money at the hotel, and he could rent a dinner jacket tomorrow, too. Of course Bolívar was waiting for him, well, let him wait, and so he left the café and took a taxi to the Battery because he wanted to touch the Statue of Liberty, according to his usual rite, and then to sit on a bench, look at the bay and the seagulls and think of Dolores. He tossed a cork into the water, filthy water, filthy pavements, even the Statue was filthy, the whole city was filthy. Two women wearing transparent plastic raincoats handed him their camera with a silent plea, then posed, with the forced smiles proper to a photograph. He framed them in the viewer, trying to include a skyscraper or two in the background, as they had indicated. Strange, he thought, that little shutter

which opened and shut like an eye, click, and transfixed a
passing moment, beyond recall, for eternity. Click. "Thank
you." "Don't mention it. Good evening." Click. A second.
Ten years gone by like a second. Dolores gone, irretrievable,
and yet she had been there only a second before, smiling
against a background of skyscrapers, at this very spot. Click:
ten years. Suddenly the ten years weighed on his shoulders,
and the fifty years of his life, as heavy as the tons of that stone
and metal colossus. Better go straight to Bolívar's and get it
over with and rent the dinner jacket on the way; it was crazy to
keep all that money around overnight, another violation of
the rules, but *they* were crazy to hand him over such a sum for
delivery. What did it mean? Were they testing his efficacy or
counting the years of his old age? A gala first performance at
the Metropolitan, a dinner jacket and thousands of dollars in
cash. Quite a joke.

It was a joke, Bolívar, I was only joking. After having been
all too imprudent he chose to make an awkward excuse.
Bolívar's big, curly-haired head, the glass-enclosed office of
the noisy workshop, the parcel tied up in brown wrapping-
paper; "Of course, old man, there has to be some joking every
now and then; by the way, how's business?" "I can't com-
plain, car accidents are on the increase, ha-ha." Bolívar. That
gypsylike face with eyes like those of a devoted dog, the
Firestone overalls, ten years of a friendship with no real
friendship to it; no questions asked, no information given,
nothing like who are you, what do you do, where are you
going, how do you live, nothing. Just a handshake, how's
business, have a cigarette, here's something for you. "But who
gives it to you, Bolívar, where do you get it, who brings it, I'd
like to know." Bolívar only stared at him with eyes wide-open,
"What sort of question is that, what's got into you?" "Nothing, really, all of a sudden I was curious, I'm growing old."
"Come now, you're a young man, Franklin." "No, I'm growing old, I know it, and they know it, too. Soon I'll be no more
use to them, they'll throw me out, you know how it goes,

Bolívar, in fact, you may be the one to get rid of me, one day you'll get the orders." "What the devil are you saying, Franklin?" "Nothing, I was joking, Bolívar. I'm in a mood for joking today. I snapped a photograph of two women tourists and with that single click of the camera ten years went by, something that can happen, you know." "I'll go with you to the door, Franklin, but by the way, is it true that they're sending you to the theatre? What theatre is it?" "What sort of a question is that, what's got into you? Questions like that are out, I'll see you another time." "I was joking, too, Franklin. *Hasta la vista.*"

*   *   *

In order to persuade the taxi driver to take him for the short distance between the hotel and the Opera House, he thrust a fifty-dollar bill under his nose. No arguments with anybody, and no running the risk of walking with all that money on him, and a dinner jacket. It would be like saying: Mugger, mug me. The driver took the money and didn't even turn on the meter. A driver of the kind that lines up in front of the Park Lane, sporting a bow tie and with good manners, one of a rare species. He got out amid the crowd. Lights making it bright as day, smart turnouts near the fountain, a social event. The entrance was already filled with people. He checked in his overcoat and scarf at the cloakroom and looked around. His contact wasn't there, so his intuition told him. He went to the foyer—an orange juice with an olive, thank you—yes, his contact was here, among the crowd. Sometimes he had singled him out at first glance, but that was in less crowded places— the library of the Hispanic Society, the toy department of Altmans, the Tourist Information Office on Times Square. He surveyed the scene. Too many people, too much light, too much red velvet. He went into the orchestra section and all the way to his seat. From this vantage point he could watch his neighbours arrive, that was an easier process. Some of his neighbours were already seated and he began to examine their faces. A Japanese, around thirty years old, with gold-rimmed glasses, an impenetrable expression, profession uncertain. A fifty-year old intellectual in the company of a fair-haired younger man with pale hands and delicate features. A middle-aged couple, the husband probably a Boston lawyer. A blonde girl sitting next to an older man, hard to say whether they were together: if so, then he was a big businessman and she was his girlfriend, they certainly weren't married, although he was wearing a wedding ring. Then two young couples, well-off newlyweds from out of town, and an old gentleman in a dinner jacket too large for him, two possibilities: either he had been on a drastic diet or else the dinner jacket was rented. Finally, a dark young man, with a close-clipped black moustache and smooth, glossy hair, a Latin-American type, took the seat next to his. The gong sounded.

And now *le roi s'amuse*. But what king and king of what? Victor Hugo's king was a king of ghosts and assumed names, he amused himself not at all. But Verdi's Duke, yes, he knew how to go about it. *Della mia incognita borghese/Toccare il fin dell'avventura io voglio*, My adventure with that unknown girl of the people I would pursue—he sang it with the self-assurance of a star aware that the evening was his: you've come from all over New York to hear me, I'm the world's greatest tenor, here's my calling-card. Immediate applause from a public easy to please, present for a social occasion. The scenery was vulgar, Mantua's ducal palace hardly good enough for a Hollywood set, too much pale pink and pale blue, terrible, really, better give your eyes a rest. He bent his head ever so slightly and looked down the row of seats. The blonde girl had put on a pair of designer glasses with fake diamonds on the stems, and seemed to be concentrating. Her probable companion seemed more distracted, his eyes were following the Contessa di Ceprano, who was crossing the stage with a lady-in-waiting: sometimes mezzo-sopranos have generous but not overflowing figures and the kind of beauty just right for a businessman in his sixties. *Anco d'Argo i cent'occhi disfido/se mi punge una qualche beltà.* The hundred eyes of Argo I defy/If a beauty strikes my eye. The Japanese had a tic in his left eye, he blinked twice in succession and then raised his eyebrow, imperceptibly, sending no clear message. The two out-of-town couples were bubbling over with happiness. One of the brides, the less ugly of the two, had a trace of lipstick at the corner of her mouth, perhaps because of the hurry to get there on time and a quick make-up in the taxi; if it were called to her attention she'd die of embarrassment. The intellectual was bored, he must have been the only one with the good taste not to care for the opera; his fair-haired companion seemed equally bored for the opposite reason. The old gentleman, on the contrary, was carried away, his lips silently forming Monterone's words, *tu che d'un padre ridi al dolore sii maledetto*, may you be cursed for laughing at a father's sorrow. Hypothesis: he was no connoisseur or he wouldn't be carried away by a performance like this one. Alternative hypothesis: he was a connoisseur of feelings, moved by Caruso and Neapolitan songs, but connoisseurs of this kind don't go to first nights at the Opera. The probable Latin-American, young and well-dressed, who looked like a heartbreaker, was equally out of tune with the opera. He seemed aware of being scrutinized and turned a receptive eye, staring back, first briefly, then at greater length. The chorus had embarked on the final aria of Scene 6, but the Duke stood above them all; *piu speme non c'è, un'ora fatale fu questa per te,* all hope is lost, this hour was fatal for you. Curtain, thundering applause. The young man looked at him again and winked, then whispered into his ear with a strong Italian accent: "His Italian is bad and, like all tenors, he's vain." He smiled back and nodded assent. Franklin, you've botched it, he said to himself, wishing he could leave.

But the scenery of the alleyway was passable, more realistic and less vulgar. The baritone was an excellent Rigoletto and a good actor as well. He asked how payment was to be made and

Sparafucile, the gun for hire, sang in answer: *Una metà si anticipa, il resto si dà poi.* Half in advance, the rest later. He turned his head around, looking down the line of faces in a quite obvious manner. The conductor was taking it very slowly, dragging everything out with long pauses! He spelled out the dialogue from his own memory, then stopped and waited. Here it was. Sparafucile laid one hand, grandiloquently, on his heart and stretched out the other arm: *Sparafucil mi nomino!* The blonde girl turned her head sideways, and their eyes met. She gave a slight nod—she had a half-smiling, malicious mouth. She transferred her attention back to the stage and did not turn again. Botched once more, Franklin. Then he thought, no, it's not possible. He slipped his hand under his jacket, the money was there, evenly distributed under the wide elastic belt; he touched it to make sure, then closed his eyes and let his thoughts wander in space and time, leaving the Opera House and the music far behind.

He waited for her on the edge of the crowd in the foyer, at the beginning of a passageway; she arrived with a trace of a smile still on her lips and walked resolutely towards him. She was the contact, no doubt of it. "Good evening, would you like a drink?" "No thanks, I'd rather do business right away; I imagine you left a box of chocolates at the cloakroom. Shall we exchange checks? If, on the other hand, you've the money on you, let's go to a telephone booth, where I can use this big evening bag. I had to look all over to find this size." Her voice was steady, indifferent. High cheekbones, brown eyes, good-looking. Thirty perhaps, or forty, hard to tell. She lit a cigarette and looked quietly at him. An easy, professional manner. "Not now," he said, "sorry, it's not the moment. At the end of the opera, if that big businessman doesn't get in the way." "What businessman?" "The one sitting next to you." "Don't be silly, I came alone, never saw him before in my life, but I don't understand why you're making me wait until the end." "You'll understand later."

*   *   *

Why, though, really? Did he really understand why? No, he
didn't, and he didn't want to think about it. Exactly. Because
I'm tired. Because I snapped a photograph. Because Dolores is
gone, because too much time has passed, because, because,
because, that's all. Because I want to have some dinner.
"Come and have dinner with me." They left their seats while
the audience was on its feet to call the tenor back to the stage.
She followed him in silence. At the cloakroom he picked up
his coat and scarf and showed her his hands, palms upward:
"Nothing up my sleeve, no chocolates. I left the money at the
hotel, if you want it, just come by, but first I'm going to have
some dinner, I'm hungry as a wolf, I've had nothing to eat
since yesterday, when I had a melted pistachio ice-cream."
"What hotel are you at?" "Never mind, if you want the money
come to dinner with me, if you're not hungry then you can
just watch me eat." She laughed and slipped her arm into his:
"Let's decide in the taxi, I opt for Lutèce, the best French
restaurant in New York. This evening deserves a French
dinner." "Fair enough." Silence in the taxi except: "It's
against the rules, you were supposed to slip the money to me
at the Opera." "True, I agree. But no more of that now. Let's
concentrate on French cooking."

They chose an inconspicuous table. "Waiter, take away all
these candles, one's enough, we want subdued light. . . Shall
we go overboard?" "Yes, let's." "Then oysters to begin with,
and champagne, not too cold." "What's your name?" "It
doesn't matter. Call me Franklin, how about you?" "Call me
what you like." "Perfect, Callmewhatyoulike is a lovely
name, more like a surname, isn't it, but whatever you say,
Callmewhatyoulike." That's the way it all starts sometimes,
with a joke, and then a conversation is sparked and carried on,
that is, if the channel is working. It was working, wine
helped. He did most of the talking: the East River, years ago,

trips to Mexico, enthusiasms, dead friends, all ghosts. "I'm tired," he said, "I'm all alone, I've had enough. . . ." Pine-apples in brandy to top it off, and two cups of coffee. "Waiter, bring me a big box of chocolates, please." He asked her to excuse him for a moment and went to the lavatory, where he threw away the chocolates and filled the box with dollars. On the way back he paid the bill, bought a rose from the cloak-room girl and laid it in the box. "Here," he said when he had come back to the table, "the very best chocolates, I had them with me the whole time. Forgive my playing games with you." She took a look inside. "Why did you do it?" "I needed company, for too many years I've been dining alone. I hope the dinner was to your taste, and now excuse me again, I'm going to bed, thanks for your company, Callmewhatyoulike, and goodnight, I doubt if we'll meet again."

As he crossed the room he left a generous tip with the waiter, *"Merci, Monsieur, au revoir,"* his legs were holding out, he was only slightly drunk, no headache, only a pleasur-able sensation. She caught up with him when he was already in the taxi, slid in beside him and said decisively, "I'm coming with you." He looked at her and she smiled. "I'm alone, too. Let's keep each other company, just for tonight." "The re-sponsibility is yours, Callmewhatyoulike. . . Driver, the Park Lane, please."

*   *   *

"Let's leave the curtains open so we can see the city by night, New York is something to see from a fortieth floor, so many lights, so many people, so many stories behind all those windows, put your arms around me, it's lovely standing here, just look at that building, it's like an ocean liner, if it were to slip anchor and take off into the night it wouldn't surprise me." "Or me either." "What's your name? Callmewhatyou-like is a surname, tell me your first name, invent it if you must." "Sparafucile's my name." "That's better Sparafucile

Callmewhatyoulike; it's been wonderful, I felt I really loved
you, a way I haven't felt for years: excuse me while I go to the
bathroom."

The bathroom lights, too bright as usual, too bright for
even a theatre dressing-room. He looked at himself in the
mirror. Under the dazzling reflector his baldness was painful
to note, but he didn't really care. He rinsed his mouth and
rubbed his forehead. He might even have whistled. Her make-
up kit lay on the marble shelf. He couldn't say why he opened
it, sometimes we make such gestures out of sheer intuition.
It's a funny feeling to find yourself in a make-up kit. But there
was his photograph, between the face powder and the mirror,
a full-length picture, captured by a telephoto lens, on the
street, somewhere or other. He held it between his thumb and
forefinger for a few seconds before he could draw any conclu-
sion. She couldn't know who he was, much less know him
personally. She wasn't supposed to. He looked hard at the
image staring out at him from the coarse-grained paper on
which pictures snapped by a telephoto lens are often printed,
an anonymous man in the crowd, the face a little thin and
drawn, Franklin. In his imagination he saw the viewfinder
framing his face and his heart. Click. While he was turning
the doorknob he thought of her big evening bag; now he knew
that there was something in it besides money; if he'd wanted
to think about it earlier he'd have realized . . . but perhaps he
hadn't wanted to think. He was sorry, he reflected, not about
the fact in itself, but about all the rest. Because it had been
wonderful. He'd have liked to tell her he was sorry that she
had to be Sparafucile; it was too bad and also funny because
everything had seemed different. But he knew he wouldn't
have time.

CINEMA

— 1 —

The small station was almost deserted. It was the station of a town on the Riviera, with palms and agaves growing near the wooden benches on the platform. At one end, behind a wrought-iron gate, a street led to the centre of the town; at the other a stone stairway went down to the shore.

The stationmaster came out of the glass-walled control room and walked under the overhanging roof to the tracks. He was a short, stout man with a moustache; he lit a cigarette, looked doubtfully at the cloudy sky, stuck out a hand beyond the roof to see if it was raining, then wheeled around and with a thoughtful air put his hands in his pockets. The two workmen waiting for the train on a bench under the sign bearing the station's name greeted him briefly and he nodded his head in reply. On the other bench there was an old woman, dressed in black, with a suitcase fastened with a rope. The stationmaster peered up and down the tracks then, as the bell announcing a train's arrival began to ring, went back into his glass-walled office.

At this moment the girl came through the gate. She was wearing a polka-dotted dress, shoes laced at the ankles, and a

pale blue sweater. She was walking quickly, as if she were
cold, and a mass of blonde hair floated under the scarf tied
around her head. She was carrying a small suitcase and a
straw handbag. One of the workmen followed her with his
eyes and nudged his apparently distracted companion. The
girl stared indifferently at the ground, then went into the
waiting room, closing the door behind her. The room was
empty. There was a large cast-iron stove in one corner and she
moved toward it, perhaps in the hope that the fire inside was
lighted. She touched it, disappointedly, and then laid her
straw handbag on top. Then she sat down on a bench and
shivered, holding her face between her hands. For a long time
she remained in this position, as if she were crying. She was
good-looking, with delicate features and slender ankles. She
took off her scarf and rearranged her hair, moving her head
from one side to the other. Her gaze wandered over the walls
of the room as if she were looking for something. There were
threatening signs on the walls addressed to the citizenry by the
Occupation Forces and notices of "wanted" persons, displaying their photographs. She looked around in confusion, then
took the handbag she had left on the stove and laid it at her
feet as if to shield it with her legs. She hunched her shoulders
and raised her jacket collar. Her hands were restless; she was
obviously nervous.

The door was flung open and a man came in. He was tall
and thin, wearing a belted tan trenchcoat and a felt hat pulled
down over his forehead. The girl leaped to her feet and
shouted, with a gurgle in her throat: "Eddie!"

He held a finger to his lips, walked toward her, and, smiling, took her into his arms. She hugged him, leaning her head
on his chest. "Oh, Eddie!" she murmured finally, drawing
back, "Eddie!"

He made her sit down and went back to the door, looking
furtively outside. Then he sat down beside her and drew some
folded papers from his pocket.

"You're to deliver them directly to the English major," he said. "Later I'll tell you how, more exactly."

She took the papers and slipped them into the opening of her sweater. She seemed fearful, and there were tears in her eyes.

"And what about you?" she asked.

He made a gesture signifying annoyance. Just then there was a rumbling sound and a freight train was visible through the door's glass panel. He pulled his hat farther down over his forehead and buried his head in a newspaper.

"Go and see what's up."

The girl went to the door and peered out. "A freight train," she said. "The two workmen sitting on the bench climbed aboard."

"Any Germans?"

"No."

The stationmaster blew his whistle and the train pulled away. The girl went back to the man and took his hands into hers.

"What about you?" she repeated.

He folded the newspaper and stuffed it into his pocket.

"This is no time to think about me," he said. "Now tell me, what's your company's schedule?"

"Tomorrow we'll be in Nice, for three evening performances. Saturday and Sunday we play in Marseille, then Montpellier and Narbonne, one day each, in short, all along the coast."

"On Sunday you'll be in Marseille," said the man. "After the show you'll receive admirers in your dressing room. Let them in one at a time. Many of them will bring flowers; some will be German spies, but others will be our people. Be sure to read the card that comes with the flowers, in the visitor's presence, every time, because I can't tell you what the contact will look like." She listened attentively; the man lit a cigarette and went on: "On one of the cards you'll read: *Fleurs pour une fleur.* Hand over the papers to that man. He'll be the major."

The bell began to ring again, and the girl looked at her watch.

"Our train will be here in a minute. Eddie, please. . ."

He wouldn't let her finish.

"Tell me about the show," he interrupted. "On Sunday night I'll try to imagine it."

"It's done by all the girls in the company," she said unenthusiastically. "Each one of us plays a well-known actress of today or of the past. That's all there is to it."

"What's the title?" he asked, smiling.

"Cinema Cinema."

"Sounds promising."

"It's a disaster," she said earnestly. "The choreography is by Savinio, just imagine that, and I play Francesca Bertini, dancing in a dress so long that I trip on it."

"Watch out!" he exclaimed jokingly. "Great tragic actresses simply mustn't fall."

Again she hid her face in her arms and started to cry. She was prettier than ever with tear marks on her face.

"Come away, Eddie, please, come away," she murmured.

He wiped her tears away gently enough, but his voice hardened, as if in an effort to disguise his feelings.

"Don't, Elsa," he said. "Try to understand." And, in a playful tone, he added: "How should I get through? Dressed like a dancer, perhaps, with a blond wig?"

The bell had stopped ringing and the incoming train could be heard in the distance. The man got up and put his hands in his pockets.

"I'll put you aboard," he said.

"No," she said, shaking her head resolutely. "You mustn't do that; it's dangerous."

"I'm doing it anyhow."

"Please!"

"One last thing," he said; "I know the major's a ladies' man. Don't smile at him too much."

She looked at him supplicatingly. "Oh, Eddie!" she exclaimed with emotion, offering him her lips.

He seemed nonplussed for a moment, as if in embarrassment or because he didn't have the courage to kiss her. Finally he deposited a fatherly kiss on her cheek.

"Stop!" called out the clapperboy. "A break!"

"Not like that!" The director's voice roared through the megaphone. "The last bit has to be done again." He was a bearded young man with a long scarf wound around his neck. Now he got down from the seat on the boom next to the camera and came to meet them. "Not like that," he repeated disappointedly. "It must be a passionate kiss, old-fashioned style, the way it was in the original film." He threw an arm around the actress's waist, bending her backwards. "Lean over her and put some passion into it," he said to the actor.

Then looking around him, he added, "Take a break!"

— 2 —

The actors invaded the station's shabby café, jostling one another in the direction of the bar. She lingered at the door, uncertain what to do, while he disappeared in the crowd. Soon he came back, precariously carrying two cups of coffee, and beckoned to her with his head to join him outside. Behind the café there was a rocky courtyard, under a vine-covered arbour, which served also for storage. Besides cases of empty bottles, there were some misshapen chairs, and on two of these they sat down, using a third one as a table.

"We're winding up," he observed.

"He insisted on doing the last scene last," she answered. "I don't know why."

"That's *modern*," he said emphatically. "Straight out of the *Cahiers du Cinema* . . . look out, that coffee's boiling hot."

"I still don't know why."

"Do they do things differently in America?" he asked.

"They certainly do!" she said with assurance. "They're less pretentious, less . . . intellectual."

"This fellow's good, though."

"It's only that, once upon a time, things weren't handled this way."

They were silent, enjoying their coffee. It was eleven in the morning, and the sea was sparkling, visible through a privet hedge around the courtyard. The vine leaves of the pergola were flaming red and the sun made shifting puddles of light on the gravel.

"A gorgeous autumn," he said, looking up at the leaves. And he added, half to himself. " 'Once upon a time' . . . Hearing you say those words had an effect on me."

She did not answer, but hugged her knees, which she had drawn up against her chest. She, too, seemed distracted, as if she had only just thought about the meaning of what she had said.

"Why did you agree to play in this film?" she asked.

"Why did *you*?"

"I don't know, but I asked you first."

"Because of an illusion," he said; "the idea of re-living . . . something like that, I suppose. I don't really know. And you?"

"I don't really know, either; with the same idea, I suppose."

The director emerged from the path which ran around the café, in good spirits and carrying a tankard of beer.

"So here are my stars!" he exclaimed, sinking into one of the misshapen chairs, with a sigh of satisfaction.

"Please spare us your speech on the beauties of direct takes," she said. "You've lectured us quite enough."

The director did not take offense at this remark and fell into casual conversation. He spoke of the film, of the importance of this new version, of why he had taken on the same actors so many years later and why he was underlining the fact that it was a remake. Things he had said many times before, as was clear from his hearers' indifference. But he enjoyed the repetition, it was almost as if he were talking to himself. He finished his beer and got up.

"Here's hoping it rains," he said as he left. "It would be too bad to shoot the last scenes with pumps." And, before turning the corner, he threw back: "Half an hour before we start shooting again."

She looked questioningly at her companion, who shook his head and shrugged his shoulders.

"It did pour during the last scene," he said, "and I was left standing in the rain."

She laughed and laid a hand on his shoulder as if to signify that she remembered.

"Do they still show it in America?" he asked with a stolid expression on his face.

"Hasn't the director projected it for our benefit exactly eleven times?" she countered, laughing. "Anyhow, in America it's shown to film clubs and other groups from time to time."

"It's the same thing here," he said. And then, abruptly: "How's the major?"

She looked at him questioningly.

"I mean Howard," he specified. "I told you not to smile at him too much, but obviously you didn't follow my advice, even if the scene isn't included in the film." And, after a moment of reflection: "I still don't understand why you married him."

"Neither do I," she said in a childlike manner. "I was very young." Her expression relaxed, as if she had put mistrust aside and given up lying. "I wanted to get even with you," she said calmly. "That was the real reason, although perhaps I wasn't aware of it. And then I wanted to go to America."

"What about Howard?" he insisted.

"Our marriage didn't last long. He wasn't right for me, really, and I wasn't cut out to be an actress."

"You disappeared completely. Why did you give up acting?"

"I couldn't get anywhere with it. After all, I'd been in just one hit, and that because of winning an audition. In America they're real pros. Once I made a series of films for television, but they were a disaster. They cast me as a disagreeable rich woman, not exactly my type, was it?"

"I think not. You look like a happy woman. Are you happy?"

"No," she said, smiling. "But I've a lot going for me."

"For instance?"

"For instance a daughter. A delightful creature, in her third university year, and we're very close."

He stared at her incredulously.

"Twenty years have gone by," she reminded him. "Nearly a lifetime."

"You're still beautiful."

"That's make-up. I have wrinkles. And I could be a grandmother."

For some time they were silent. Voices from the café drifted out to them, and someone started up the jukebox. He looked as if he were going to speak, but stared at the ground, seemingly at a loss for words.

"I want you to tell me about your life," he said at last. "All through the filming I've wanted to ask you, but I've got around to it only now."

"Certainly," she said, spiritedly. "And I'd like to hear you talk about yours."

At this juncture the production secretary appeared in the doorway, a thin, homely, plaintive young woman with her hair in a ponytail and a pair of glasses on her nose.

"Make-up time!" she called out. "We start shooting in ten minutes."

— 3 —

The bell stopped ringing and the incoming train could be heard in the distance. The man got up and put his hands in his pockets.

"I'll put you aboard," he said.

"No," she said, shaking her head resolutely. "You mustn't do that, it's dangerous."

"I'm doing it anyhow."

"Please!"

"One last thing," he said, "I know the major's a ladies' man. Don't smile at him too much."

She looked at him supplicatingly. "Oh, Eddie!" she exclaimed with emotion, offering him her lips.

He put his arm around her waist, bending her backwards. Looking into her eyes, he slowly advanced his mouth towards her and gave her a passionate kiss, a long, intense kiss, which aroused an approving murmur and some catcalls.

"Stop!" called the clapperboy. "End of scene."

"Lunchtime," the director announced through the megaphone. "Back at four o'clock."

The actors dispersed in various directions, some to the café, others to trailers parked in front of the station. He took off his trenchcoat and hung it over his arm. They were the last to arrive on the street, where they set out towards the sea. A blade of sunlight struck the row of pink houses along the harbour, and the sea was of a celestial, almost diaphanous blue. A woman with a tub under her arm appeared on a balcony and began to hang up clothes to dry. Then she grasped a pulley and the clothes slid along a line from one house to another, fluttering like flags. The houses formed the arches of a portico and underneath there were stalls, covered during the midday break with oilcloth. Some bore painted blue anchors and a sign saying *Fresh Fish*.

"There used to be a pizzeria here," he said, "I remember it perfectly, it was called *Da Pezzi*."

She looked at the paving-stones and did not speak.

"You *must* remember," he continued. "There was a sign 'Pizza to take out,' and I said to you: 'Let's purchase a pizza from Pezzi,' and you laughed."

They went down the steps of a narrow alley with windows joined by an arch above them. The echo of their footsteps on the shiny paving-stones conveyed a feeling of winter, with the crackling tone that sounds acquire in cold air. Actually there was a warm breeze and the fragrance of mock-orange. The shops on the waterfront were closed and café chairs were stacked up around empty tables.

"We're out of season," she observed.

He shot her a surreptitious look, wondering if the remark had a double meaning, then let it go.

"There's a restaurant that's open," he said, gesturing with his head. "What do you say?"

The restaurant was called *L'Arsella*; it was a wood and glass construction resting on piles set into the beach next to the blue bathhouses. Two gently rocking boats were tied to the piles. Some windows had blinds drawn over them; lamps were lit on the tables in spite of the bright daylight. There were few customers: a couple of silent, middle-aged Germans, two intellectual-looking young men, a woman with a dog, the last summer vacationers. They sat down at a corner table, far from the others. Perhaps the waiter recognized them; he came quickly but with an embarrassed and would-be confidential air. They ordered broiled sole and champagne and looked out at the horizon, which changed colour as wind pushed the clouds around. Now there was a hint of indigo on the line separating sea and sky, and the promontory that closed the bay was silvery green like a block of ice.

"Incredible," she said after a minute or two, "only three weeks to shoot a film, ridiculous, I call it. We've done some scenes only once."

"That's avant-garde," he said, smiling. "Fake realism, *cinéma-vérité*, they call it. Today's production costs are high, so they do everything in a hurry." He was making bread crumbs into little balls and lining them up in front of his plate. "Anghelopoulos," he said ironically. "He'd like to do a film like *O Thiassos*, a play within a play, with us acting ourselves. Period songs and accessories and transitional sequences, all very well, but what's to take the place of myth and tragedy?"

The waiter brought on the champagne and uncorked the bottle. She raised her glass as if in a toast. Her eyes were malicious and shiny, full of reflections.

"Melodrama," she said, "Melodrama, that's what." She took short sips and broke into a smile. "That's why he wanted the acting overdone. We had to be caricatures of ourselves."

He raised his glass in return. "Then hurrah for melodrama!" he said. "Sophocles, Shakespeare, Racine, they all go in for it. That's what I've been up to myself all these years."

"Talk to me about yourself," she said.

"Do you mean it?"

"I do."

"I have a farm in Provence, and I go there when I can. The countryside is just hilly enough, people are welcoming, and I like horses."

He made more bread-crumb balls, two circles of them around a glass, and then he moved one behind the other as if he were playing patience.

"That's not what I meant," she said.

He called the waiter and ordered another bottle of champagne.

"I teach at the Academy of Dramatic Arts," he said. "My life's made up of Creon, Macbeth, Henry VIII." He gave a guilty smile. "Hardhearted fellows, all."

She looked at him intently, with a concentrated, almost anxious air.

"What about films?" she asked.

"Five years ago I was in a mystery story. I played an American private detective, just three scenes, and then they bumped me off in an elevator. But in the titles they ran my name in capital letters . . . 'With the participation of . . .'"

"You're a myth," she said emphatically.

"A leftover," he demurred. "I'm this butt between my lips, see . . ." He put on a hard, desperate expression and let the smoke from the cigarette hanging between his lips cover his face.

"Don't play Eddie!" she said, laughing.

"But I *am* Eddie," he muttered, pulling an imaginary hat over his eyes. He refilled the glasses and raised his.

"To films and filmmaking!"

"If we go on like this we'll be drunk when we go back to the set, *Eddie*." She stressed the name, and there was a malicious glint in her eyes.

He took off the imaginary hat and laid it over his heart.

"Better that way. We'll be more melodramatic."

For a sweet they had ordered ice-cream with hot chocolate sauce. The waiter arrived with a triumphal air, bearing a tray with ice-creams in one hand and the steaming chocolate sauce in the other. While serving them he asked, timidly but coyly, if they would honour him with their autographs on a menu and shot them a gratified smile when they assented.

The ice-cream was in the shape of a flower, with deep red cherries at the centre of the corolla. He picked one of these up with his fingers and carried it to his mouth.

"Look here," he said. "Let's change the ending."

She looked at him, seemingly perplexed, but perhaps her

look signified that she knew what he was driving at and was merely awaiting confirmation.

"Don't go," he said. "Stay here with me."

She lowered her eyes to her plate as if in embarrassment.

"Please," she said, "please."

"You're talking the way you do in the film," he said. "That's the exact line."

"We're not in a film now," she said, almost resentfully. "Stop playing your part; you're overdoing it."

He made a gesture that seemed to signify dropping the whole thing.

"But I love you," he said in a low voice.

She put on a teasing tone.

"Of course," she said, in slightly haughty fashion, "in the film."

"It's the same thing," he said. "It's all a film."

"All what's a film?"

"Everything." He stretched his hand across the table and squeezed hers. "Let's run the film backwards and go back to the beginning."

She looked at him as if she didn't have the courage to reply. She let him stroke her hand and stroked his in return.

"You've forgotten the title of the film," she said, trying for a quick retort. "'Point of No Return.'"

The waiter arrived, beaming and waving a menu for them to autograph.

— 4 —

"You're mad!" she said laughing, but letting him pull her along. "They'll be furious."

He pulled her onto the pier and quickened his steps.

"Let them be furious," he said. "Let that cock-of-the-walk wait. Waiting makes for inspiration."

There were no more than a dozen people on the boat, scattered on the benches in the cabin and on the iron seats, painted white, at the stern. Their dress and casual behaviour marked them as local people, used to this crossing. Three women were carrying plastic bags bearing the name of a well-known shop. Plainly they had come from villages on the perimeter of the bay to make purchases in the town. The employee who punched the tickets was wearing blue trousers and a white shirt with the company seal sewed onto it. The actor asked how long it would take to make the round trip. The ticket-collector made a sweeping gesture and enumerated the villages where they would be stopping. He was a young man with a blond moustache and a strong local accent.

"About an hour and a half," he said, "but if you're in a hurry, there's a larger boat which returns to the mainland from our first stop, just after we arrive, and will bring you back in forty minutes."

He pointed to the first village on the north side of the bay.

She still seemed undecided, torn between doubt and temptation.

"They'll be furious," she repeated. "They wanted to wrap it up by evening."

He shrugged his shoulders and threw up his hands.

"If we don't finish today we'll finish tomorrow," he countered. "We're paid for the job, not by the hour, so we can surely take an extra half-day."

"I've a plane for New York tomorrow," she said. "I made a reservation, and my daughter will be waiting for me."

"Lady, make up your mind," said the ticket-collector. "We have to push off."

A whistle blew twice and a sailor started to release the mooring rope. The ticket-collector pulled out his pad and tore off two tickets.

"You'll be better off at the bow," he remarked. "There's a bit of breeze, but you won't feel the rolling."

The seats were all free, but they leaned on the low railing and looked at the scene around them. The boat drew away from the pier and gathered speed. From a slight distance the town revealed its exact layout, with the old houses falling into an unexpected and graceful geometrical pattern.

"It's more beautiful viewed from the sea," she observed. She held down her windblown hair with one hand, and red spots had appeared on her cheekbones.

"You're the beauty," he said, "at sea, on land, and wherever."

She laughed and searched her bag for a scarf.

"You've turned very gallant," she said. "Once upon a time you weren't like that at all."

"Once upon a time I was stupid, stupid and childish."

"Actually, you seem more childish to me now than then. Forgive me for saying so, but that's what I think."

"You're wrong, though. I'm older, that's all." He shot her a worried glance. "Now don't tell me I'm old."

"No, you're not old. But that's not the only thing that matters."

She took a tortoiseshell case out of her bag and extracted a cigarette. He cupped his hands around hers to protect the match from the wind. The sky was very blue, although there was a black streak on the horizon and the sea had darkened. The first village was rapidly approaching. They could see a pink bell tower and a bulging spire as white as meringue. A flight of pigeons rose up from the houses and took off, describing a wide curve towards the sea.

"Life must be wonderful there," he said, "and very simple."

She nodded and smiled.

"Perhaps because it's not ours."

The boat they were to meet was tied up at the pier, an old boat looking like a tug. For the benefit of the new arrival it whistled three times in greeting. Several people were standing on the pier, perhaps waiting to go aboard. A little girl in a yellow dress, holding a woman's hand, was jumping up and down like a bird.

"That's what I'd like," he said inconsequentially. "To live a life other than ours."

From her expression he saw that his meaning was not clear and corrected himself.

"I mean a happy life rather than ours, like the one we imagine they lead in this village."

He grasped her hands and made her meet his eyes, looking at her very hard.

She gently freed herself, giving him a rapid kiss.

"Eddie," she said tenderly, "dear Eddie." Slipping her arm into his she pulled him towards the gangplank. "You're a great actor," she said, "a truly great actor." She was happy and brimming over with life.

"But it's what I feel," he protested feebly, letting her pull him along.

"Of course," she said, "like a true actor."

— 5 —

The train came to a sudden stop, with the wheels screeching and puffs of smoke rising from the engine. A compartment opened and five girls stuck out their heads. Some of them were peroxide blondes, with curls falling over their shoulders and on their foreheads. They started to laugh and chat, calling out: "Elsa! Elsa!" A showy redhead, wearing a green ribbon in her hair, shouted to the others: "There she is!" and leaned even farther out to wave her hands in greeting. Elsa quickened her step and came close to the window, touching the gaily outstretched hands.

"Corinna!" she exclaimed, looking at the redhead, "What's this get-up?"

"Saverio says it's attractive," Corinna called back, winking and pointing her head towards the inside of the compartment. "Come on aboard," she added in a falsetto voice; "you don't want to be stuck in a place like this, do you?" Then, suddenly, she screamed: "Look girls, there's a Rudolph Valentino!"

The girls waved madly to catch the man's attention. Eddie had come out from behind the arrivals and departures board; he advanced slowly along the platform, with his hat pulled over his eyes. At that same moment, two German soldiers came through the gate and went towards the stationmaster's office. After a few moments the stationmaster came out with his red flag under his arm and walked towards the engine, with rapid steps, which accentuated the awkwardness of his chubby body. The soldiers stood in front of the office door, as if they were on guard. The girls fell silent and watched the scene looking worried. Elsa set down her suitcase and looked confusedly at Eddie, who motioned with his head that she should go on. Then he sat down on a bench, under a tourist poster, took the newspaper out of his pocket and buried his face in it. Corinna seemed to understand what was up.

"Come on, dearie!" she shouted. "Come aboard!"

With one hand she waved at the two staring soldiers and gave them a dazzling smile. Meanwhile the stationmaster was coming back with the flag now rolled up under his arm. Corinna asked him what was going on.

"Don't ask me," he answered, shrugging his shoulders. "It seems we have to wait for a quarter of an hour. It's orders, that's all I know."

"Then we can get out and stretch our legs, girls," Corinna chirped. "Climb aboard," she whispered as she passed Elsa. "We'll take care of them."

The little group moved in the direction opposite to where Eddie was seated, passing in front of the soldiers. "Isn't there anywhere to eat in this station?" Corinna asked in a loud voice, looking around. She was superb at drawing attention to herself, swinging her hips and also the bag she had taken off her shoulder. She had on a clinging flowered dress and sandals with cork soles.

"The sea, girls!" she shouted. "Look at that sea and tell me
if it isn't divine!" She leaned theatrically against the first
lamp-post and raised her hand to her mouth, putting on a
childish manner. "If I had my bathing suit with me, I'd dive,
never mind the autumn weather," she said, tossing her head
and causing her red curls to ripple over her shoulders.

The two soldiers were stunned and couldn't take their eyes
off her. Then she had a stroke of genius, due to the lamp-post,
perhaps, or to the necessity of resolving an impossible situation. She let her blouse slip down off her shoulders, leaned
against the lamp-post, stretched out her arms and addressed
an imaginary public, winking as if the whole scene were in
cahoots with her.

"It's a song they sing the world over," she shouted, "even
our enemies!" And, turning to the other girls, she clapped
her hands. It must have been part of the show, because they
fell into line, raising their legs in marching time but without
moving an inch, their hands at their foreheads in a military
salute. Corinna clung to the lamp-post with one hand
and, using it as a pivot, wheeled gracefully around it, while
her skirt, fluttering in the breeze, displayed her legs to advan-
tage.

> *"Vor der Kaserne vor dem grossen Tor,*
> *Stand eine Laterne, und steht sie noch davor . . .*
> *So wollen wir uns da wiedersehen,*
> *Bei der Laterne wollen wir stehen,*
> *Wie einst Lili Marlene, wie einst Lili Marlene."*

The girls applauded and one of the soldiers whistled.
Corinna thanked them with a mock bow and went to the
fountain near the hedge. She passed a wet finger over her
forehead while looking down at the street below; then, trailed
by the other girls, she started to reboard the train.

"Goodbye, boys!" she shouted to the soldiers. "We're going
to snatch some rest. We've a long tour ahead of us."

Elsa was waiting in the corridor and threw her arms around her.

"You're an angel, Corinna," she said, giving her a kiss.

"Think nothing of it," said Corinna, starting to cry like a baby.

The two soldiers had come close to the waiting train; they looked up at the girls and tried to exchange words; one of them knew some Italian. Just then there was the sound of a motor, and a black car came through the gate and travelled the length of the platform until it stopped at the front, just behind the engine. The girls tried to fathom what was happening, but there was a curve in the tracks and they couldn't see very well around it. Eddie hadn't moved from the bench. Apparently he was immersed in the newspaper that shielded his face.

"What's up?" asked Elsa, trying to seem indifferent as she stowed her things in the luggage net.

"Nothing," one of the girls answered. "It must be a big shot who arrived in the car. He's in civilian clothes and travelling first-class."

"Is he alone?" Elsa asked.

"It seems so. The soldiers are standing at attention and not boarding the train."

Elsa peered out the window. The soldiers had turned around and were walking towards the road leading into the town. The stationmaster came back, dragging the red flag behind him and looking down at his shoes.

"The train's leaving," he said in a philosophical, knowing manner, and waved the flag. The engine whistled. The girls returned to their seats, only Elsa stayed at the window. She had combed her hair off her forehead and her eyes were still gleaming. At this moment Eddie came up and stood directly under the window.

"Goodbye, Eddie," Elsa murmured, stretching out her hand.

"Shall we meet in another film?" he asked.

"What the devil is he saying?" shouted the director from behind him. "What the devil?"

"Shall I hold?" asked the cameraman.

"No," said the director. "It's going to be dubbed anyhow." And he shouted into the megaphone, "Walk, man, the train's moving, move faster, follow it along the platform, hold her hand."

The train had, indeed, started, and Eddie obeyed orders, quickening his pace and keeping up as long as he could. The train picked up speed and went around the curve and through a switch on the other side. Eddie wheeled about and took a few steps before stopping to light a cigarette and then walk slowly on into camera. The director made gestures to regulate his pace, as if he were manipulating him with strings.

"Insert a heart attack," said Eddie imploringly.

"What do you mean?"

"A heart attack," Eddie repeated. "Here, on the bench. I'll look exhausted, sink onto the bench and lay my hand on my heart like Dr. Zhivago. Make me die."

The clapperboy looked at the director, waiting for instructions.

The director moved his fingers like scissors to signify that he'd cut later, but meanwhile the shooting must go on.

"What do you mean by a heart attack?" he said to Eddie. "Do you think you look like a man about to have a heart attack? Pull your hat over your eyes, like a good Eddie, don't make me start all over." And he signalled to the crew to put the pumps into action. "Come on, move! It's starting to rain. You're Eddie, remember, not a poor lovelorn creature . . . Put your hands in your pockets, shrug your shoulders, that's it, good boy, come towards us . . . your cigarette hanging from your lips . . . perfect! . . . eyes on the ground."

He turned to the cameraman and shouted: "Pull back—tracking shot; pull back!"